BLIND ITEMS

Kate McMurray

Dreamspinner Press

Published by
Dreamspinner Press
4760 Preston Road
Suite 244-149
Frisco, TX 75034
http://www.dreamspinnerpress.com/

Blind Items
Copyright © 2011 by Kate McMurray

Cover Art by Reese Dante   http://www.reesedante.com

ISBN: 978-1-61372-068-4

Printed in the United States of America
First Edition
July 2011

eBook edition available
eBook ISBN: 978-1-61372-069-1

To Jon, with whom I once spent
many afternoons at the mall food court.
And to the NYC writers group
for all of their amazing generosity and support.

CHAPTER
One

TWICE in my life, I've walked into a situation and known everything was about to change.

I was thirteen the first time. I walked into Mrs. Pearl's classroom on the first day of eighth grade and scanned the rows of desks to find prime real estate. I saw an empty desk right in the middle, and as I made my way towards it, I noticed a dark-haired boy I'd never seen before sitting at the desk next to it. And I just... *knew*. The hairs on the back of my neck stood up. Oblivious, he stared forlornly out the window.

I slid into the empty desk. "Are you new?" I asked him.

He blinked and turned toward me. I almost fell out of my chair as I realized how handsome he was. He gave me a brief once-over before eyeing my shirt warily. It's possible I was wearing a bright turquoise shirt with the collar popped up. It was the early nineties, I was thirteen, I don't know. He said, "Yeah, I'm new."

"Cool. New to town or what?"

"No, I...." Then he stopped talking.

"You what?"

"I went to Harlan Prep before this."

We public school kids had made an occupation of making fun of the kids who went to the tony prep school a few towns over. This kid did not strike me as the prep-school type. He looked too Latino, for one thing; I know how that sounds, but it was fairly common knowledge that Harlan Prep looked basically like the headquarters for the Aryan Nation. In other words, it surprised me that this guy was a prep-school refugee, but then I realized I was sitting next to an expensively appointed kid, that the shirt he had on probably cost more than every piece of clothing on my body combined. "Oh," I said.

"But I mean, I didn't flunk out or anything. I wanted to come to public school."

I laughed, more out of nervousness than anything else. He really was a good-looking guy. "Good Lord, why?"

He shrugged. "Cuz I'm not like them."

I assumed he meant the other kids at Harlan, so I didn't question him. I had some guesses about why. That, and not being like the other kids was a feeling with which I was familiar. Instead, I said, "Well, welcome to hell. I'm Drew, and I'm happy to be your tour guide."

He chuckled. "I'm Rey."

And with a handshake, our fates were sealed.

BECAUSE he was handsome and charming, it didn't take Rey long to become the toast of the school, the guy everybody wanted to be friends with. I couldn't tell you why—maybe it was some kind of blind allegiance formed because I was the first person who reached out to him at his new school—but he stuck by me all through that year and beyond. When we were freshmen in high school, someone wrote "GAY!" on my locker in black marker, which led to other kids contributing other fun words in pink spray-paint and leaving a purple feather boa draped over the combination lock.

The perpetrator of the original crime was a not-especially-smart member of our class, so it didn't take much for us to find him. We had a confrontation one afternoon during which the kid started calling me all manner of horrible names. Rey offered to beat him up, but I didn't want to cause more trouble, so I told him not to, right there in the hallway in front of a dozen other students. Rey punched the kid anyway, giving him a bloody nose. I draped the feather boa around my neck like an Olympic medal. Nobody messed with me for the rest of the school year.

WE BOTH had crappy parents. In retrospect, that seems an odd thing to base a friendship on, but I think that we found something in each other that was lacking at home.

Rey was talking his father into letting him go to public school the same summer my father finally took off. *Good riddance*, I thought at the time. My dad was the kind of pop psychologist who did guest shots on talk shows a lot. The key to his success was tilting his head and looking sympathetic. For extra fun, he'd relate his own experiences to his patients, but often these were experiences he'd never actually had. He talked a good game on TV about how to raise kids, but his parenting ever since that summer he walked out mostly involved sending me cards on my birthday. To this day, I still get a card, often a few days late, with a ten-dollar bill stuck in it like I'm a fucking five-year-old. And I'll never forget when, about a month after I came out to him, my father was on an episode of *Oprah* about parents struggling with their children's sexual identities. He actually said the words, "I have a gay son, so I understand what you're going through." I wanted to shout and throw things at him. I did, in fact, pull off my shoe and toss it at the screen. It bounced off and lay impotently on the floor. "You don't know shit!" I shouted at the TV. Mom ran in then to find out what the commotion was, but all she had to see was her ex-husband's face. "That man," she mumbled. She gave me a kiss on the cheek before leaving the room again.

Rey's absentee parent was his mother. Rey called her a "free spirit," which I think was his code for "flakier than a croissant." After his parents split up when he was five, she would flit and flitter in and out of his life, usually to swoop in and play The Cool Mom for a week or so before taking off again. I adored her when I was a teenager—she told these completely insane stories about her travels around the world and she let us drink beer—but it took me a while to understand what her long absences did to Rey. His father wasn't much better. He meant well and obviously loved his son, but he owned North Jersey's largest manufacturer of toilet paper and paper towels, a job that kept him busy upwards of seventy hours a week.

I at least had my mother, who was probably the best parent a boy could have asked for. She went a little above and beyond when I told her I was gay, joining PFLAG and buying me boxes of condoms long before I was ready to do anything with them, but she was always accepting and supportive. I suspected at the time that this was why Rey started spending the night at my place with increasing frequency. I couldn't figure out why he wanted to stay in my dilapidated old house when he lived in this gorgeous mansion on the other side of town, but then, I always preferred to sleep at my house too.

OF COURSE now, all these years later, he's not just Rey, he's Reynolds Blethwyn, star of stage and screen, and the summer we both turned thirty, he was on everyone's radar. He wrapped the third season of his hit evening soap and then flew off to the Czech Republic to film an action movie. The press loved him to pieces.

The press also loved a juicy bit of gossip, which meant that as Rey's star rose, so too did the frequency with which his name appeared in conjunction with some crazy rumor. Rey was pretty good at letting it all roll off his back, but I found the whole experience kind of surreal. Then again, I knew all about worshipping at the altar of Reynolds Blethwyn; I'd been doing it longer than anyone. *Sure*, I'd think when I saw the gossip rags on the newsstand, *you all love him now. But I loved him first.*

It was an altogether different rumor, though, that really got me into hot water that fall. The fallout from that rumor was the second time in my life that I knew everything was about to change.

CHAPTER
Two

THE whole mess began with my fluke television appearance.

Or, it wasn't that much of a fluke. I was invited to be on *News Night with Libby Madden* as a lefty talking head, my only real qualification for which was that I wrote a column for an underground rag called *The New York Forum*. Libby and I went way back, though; she and I had both lived on the same block in the Fort Greene neighborhood of Brooklyn for a while and had been involved in the same community garden project. We argued over hydrangeas but then got to be friends. We'd kept in touch after she moved to Manhattan and got the job at *News Night*. Whenever there was a big gay rights story in the news, she called me, and if I was available, I'd go on the show to make quips. Probably it didn't hurt that I was not unattractive; I was young and in good shape, with clear skin and untamable brown hair. I didn't do the TV gig often, though; being on TV freaked me out, frankly.

But I agreed this time mostly because one of my pet column topics was in the news. There was speculation that Richard Granger, the senior senator from Kansas, was planning to run for president.

They put some makeup on me and sat me in a chair at the news desk, and I tried to keep from giggling as Libby introduced me: "Here with me now is writer and activist Andrew Walsh. How are you, Drew?"

"I'm great, Libby."

I did a five-minute segment toward the end of the show in which I mostly spouted off (with lots of puns; that's why they paid me) about how offensive I found Granger. The latest bit of shenanigans was that he'd come out against an employment non-discrimination act aimed at making it illegal to fire employees for being gay. In the end, he was able to keep his disdain for the homosexual population under wraps, but he did say publicly that employers should have the right to hire and fire whoever they wanted, and if some bigoted asshole (I'm paraphrasing) wanted to keep his company a rainbow-free zone, that was his prerogative. Libby implied during the segment that she thought Granger was too conservative to gain any traction with mainstream America, but I had my doubts, probably born mostly of paranoia.

But, you know, the thing with having a job where you get paid to write (and sometimes say aloud) your opinion is that you tend to forget that the people you're writing about are real, with minutiae-ridden daily lives and families. I'd vilified Granger to cartoon-villain proportions. I kind of forgot he was a real man.

At the end of the segment, Libby made a joke implying that Granger probably sucked cock on the side. Well, what she actually said was, "Have you noticed the trend with anti-gay politicians and the men they keep in their closets?" It had become a running gag; Libby contended on her show often that if a politician was vehemently against something, he was probably doing it, and anyone who protested homosexuality as loudly as Granger did was probably gay. He wasn't, as it turned out, but Libby couldn't have known how close her words got to the truth.

I HAD to go see my editor a few days later. I always thought the *Forum*'s newsroom was like a big medieval maze. There were cubicle walls instead of hedges, but all the same, I found it impossible to navigate. I stood at one end and all eyes rose to look at me, seeming to silently dare me to try my luck at getting through the maze, with fax machines and copiers standing in my way as obstacles. Luckily, just as quickly, the eyes went back to their own work, leaving me to ponder how, exactly, I was supposed to get from my end of the maze to my editor's desk at the other side. This was why I was freelance. I'd never be cut out for a nine-to-five job.

I followed an assistant who deftly made her way around stray equipment and desks, and finally, we arrived at Wade Warren's office.

"Mr. Walsh is here," the assistant announced before stranding me there. I started to panic about how to get out again, but then Wade beckoned for me to sit.

"Thank you for coming in, Andrew," he said. "Try to look less terrified."

I managed to laugh weakly before sitting in the worn-out chair across from Wade's desk. Everything looked a little worn; circulation was down, so the *Forum* was not exactly a well-funded operation. "I'm sorry," I said. "Every time I come here, everything moves around. I don't know how you find your office every day. I'd have to leave breadcrumbs."

Wade smiled indulgently but went into all-business mode. "I saw you on TV the other night."

I laughed nervously. "I wasn't a *complete* disaster, was I?"

He pulled a file folder out from under his blotter and handed it to me. "Not quite, no." He cleared his throat. "I mentioned on the phone that I think you're the right man to do this feature for us."

I nodded. "Sure, but I'm still not sure why. I haven't done a feature for you guys in a while."

Wade sat back in his chair. "Look, you know that your column is one of our most popular. I'm not gonna lie. I think you, Alex on music, and that damn advice columnist...." Wade folded his hands on his desk and shook his head. I'd heard Wade's rant on the uselessness of advice columns before, so I waited for him to go on. "You guys account for most of our circulation. I think a story like this has to be covered by someone our readers know."

"All right." I was starting to feel intimidated. I didn't like the idea of a big story. Just having the column had gotten me into enough trouble in the five years I'd been doing it. And while I appreciated that the *Forum* paid me to write and gave me a lot of freedom, I didn't really want to get in any deeper. Still, my curiosity was piqued. "What's the story?" I asked.

Wade pointed to the folder. I opened it. There was what looked like a yearbook photo of a blond guy in his early twenties clipped to three typewritten pages. Wade said, "You know Senator Granger from Kansas?"

Ha. I gave Wade my best "You've got to be kidding" look.

"That's his son Jonathan."

Surprised, I looked at the photo again. I'd had the misfortune of meeting Richard Granger in person once—he was Rey's uncle, and how's *that* for a coincidence?—so I had a good idea of what the man looked like up close. I supposed there was a vague resemblance between that man and the guy in the photo. "All right," I said. "So?"

"So, the kid's come to town to be a teacher. Just finished his master's, got a job teaching science in the New York public school system."

"Of course he did."

"So we want you to do a feature on him. Interview him, follow him around for a day, find out what makes him tick, why he's in New York."

This still wasn't making any sense. "I imagine he's teaching to show that his father is so wonderful, he raised a great, wholesome, self-sacrificing son." I shook my head. "I don't get it. This is hardly my kind of story. Why not toss it to one of the features editors?" More to the point, I couldn't figure out why the *Forum*, an alt-weekly known mostly for cultural criticism and its tendency towards the salacious, would be interested in such a bland story. I studied Granger Junior's photo and tried to puzzle it out.

"I have a source that says he's gay."

I looked up. That was the angle, of course. Wouldn't it be perfect if the senator, one of the most conservative, anti-gay politicians in Washington, had a gay son? And wouldn't I, the

Forum's token gay—or "culture columnist," as Wade referred to me—be the perfect man to write the story? "I see," I said.

I flipped through the pages in the folder to see if a source for Wade's rumor was listed, but he reached across the desk and closed the folder. As if he knew what I was after, he said, "I can't tell you the source, I swore to him his name wouldn't get out."

Frustrated, I looked at the folder in my hands. "So… what? You know I don't have a lot of feature-writing experience. What do I do? Follow him around, ask him how rewarding his teaching experience is, then just casually ask him if he's gay? Invite him to a gay bar and see if he says yes? Or just take it on faith that what you say is true? I don't think so, Wade. Not to mention that, if he's not gay or won't admit that he is, having my name on the story's byline automatically implies that someone sure as hell thinks he is. I can't do that to the guy, especially if your source is wrong. I don't care who his father is."

"Come on, Andrew, you're not just a columnist at the *Forum*, you're a great writer, a journalist! You write for other media, right?"

"Well, yeah, but…."

"So here's your big break. You want to disregard his connection to Senator Granger, then fine, be impartial. Go meet the guy, find out what his deal is. Maybe there's no story, maybe you write a sweet story about the son of a man you've publicly excoriated making good. Or maybe this is the story I think it is and you get credit for breaking it."

The whole thing left a bad taste in my mouth. "I don't think I want that credit."

"Think about it. At least meet Jonathan Granger or give him a call. His contact info is all in that folder. If you don't think you can do the story, no harm. All right?"

"All right." I knew it was a mistake to agree to the story, but it was hard to say no to Wade, and I kind of needed the paycheck anyway. "Give me a couple of days. I'll let you know."

THE venue had changed, but the sentiment was the same. At sixteen, the location had been our regular table near the fast-food chicken place in the food court at the Paramus Park Mall; at thirty, the venue was a café on Seventh Avenue in Park Slope, Brooklyn. Either way, it was a Crisis Lunch.

I walked into the café and found Rey already seated. As sometimes happened after I hadn't seen him in a while, I felt sucker-punched when I saw him. All that black hair, the square jaw, the chiseled body. Let's put it this way: he hadn't been cast as the love interest in a popular TV drama just for his acting abilities.

I walked to the table and considered giving him a hug. Instead, I sat and opted for a manly handshake. "Welcome back to civilization," I said.

He chuckled. "Hi. Prague is plenty civilized."

"Oh, sure, but it's not New York."

"That's true, but what else is?" He fiddled with the napkin in front of him. "Seriously, though, I feel good about this movie."

"Well, that's good. I'd hate for my $12.50 to go to waste."

"Right. Like you aren't going to try to wheedle tickets to the premiere out of me."

I grinned. "Well, the part I'm most looking forward to is watching you pretend to be an action hero."

"I'll have you know that I'm a great action hero." He puffed out his chest.

"Sure." I laughed. "I missed you, man. I'm glad you're back in New York."

"Yeah. I really liked Prague, though. I wish I could have spent more time there, actually. Most of the filming we did was quite a few miles out of town. It's a lovely city, though. You should go see it sometime."

"All right. I'll add it to the list of places to see before I die." I smiled at Rey and waited a moment. "So, before the main course arrives, I have a favor to ask."

Rey furrowed his brow. "No good ever came from those words out of your mouth."

"Now, hey, this is not a difficult favor. So, you have a cousin Jonathan."

"He called the other night to say we should go out. So now it's not just Uncle Richard."

"What do you mean?"

Rey sighed. "Jonny just moved here. My uncle has been pestering me ever since he arrived. Richard thinks I should take Jonny out on the town, introduce him to the city. Jonny was always kind of a stick in the mud, though, so I haven't gotten around to agreeing to take him out."

"Ah, family."

"Yeah, well." Rey took a sip of coffee. "I mean, I'll take him out for a beer or something eventually."

"So funny thing about that. I've been assigned to write a story on him."

"What?" Rey frowned again. "A story? About my cousin Jonny?"

"A story about Jonathan Granger, the senator's son who came to New York to teach the rough-and-tumble inner-city youth. Only he's teaching honors physics at Brooklyn Tech, so he's got some things to learn about inner-city youth, I imagine."

"But that doesn't make any sense. Why give you the story?"

It was going to be hard, breaking this to Rey. "Well, exactly. That's what I said to my editor at the *Forum*. And you know what he said to me?"

"What?"

"A source says he's gay."

Rey laughed. "No way."

"I'm just telling you what my editor told me. I figured I'd run it by you, see what you thought. I suspected it was wishful thinking on Wade Warren's part, his typical MO of looking for a story where none exists. But, seeing as he's your cousin, I thought you might know either way."

"He doesn't set off my gaydar."

I sipped my water. "Honey, please. Your gaydar never worked properly."

Rey grimaced. "I really don't think he's gay. If he was, don't you think there'd be a big scandal?"

"That's exactly what Wade's hoping for."

Rey shook his head. The waitress came over and took our orders. After she left, I picked up the paper someone had discarded on the neighboring table. It was the *Post*, unfortunately, but I flipped through it anyway until I found something interesting. "Well, well. You made Page Six." I handed the paper to Rey. "Says you were spotted at a bar in the Village and went home with some brunette two nights ago. Did you?"

"No," he said. "I didn't even leave my apartment that night."

"Sure." I didn't believe it for a moment. Rey was on the rebound from a fairly awful breakup and seemed to be sleeping with every woman who walked past him. "I guess you know you've arrived if Page Six is making up shit about you."

"Beats the gay rumors, I guess."

"What's that supposed to mean?"

"Nothing." Rey took a roll from the basket on the table and contemplated it. "I mean, no offense. But you saw the rumors a few months ago. All it takes is someone misreading a stupid blind item on a gossip blog and everyone's off to the races. Reynolds Blethwyn's secret gay lover confesses, or whatever the shit that was. You know that I don't care. But my handlers don't like rumors like that. No one takes a gay leading man seriously."

"But you're not gay," I said. This was a fact I probably knew better than anybody.

"And no amount of people saying it will make it true. But success in this industry is all about other people's perceptions."

This whole conversation made me a little sad. "Well, then, I'll amend what I said earlier. You're officially a sex symbol when the gay rumors start."

"Yeah," Rey said. "Let the press say what it wants."

I suspected Rey was lying about not caring, but I let it go. "Good thing they've got you paired with a mystery woman now. Are you seeing someone?"

"No, not really. What about you? Anything interesting happen while I was out of town?"

"Nada."

"You're not still avoiding Aaron, are you? You realize that by not going to 'your places', you effectively cut yourself off from ninety percent of the gay population in this city, which decreases your odds of ever getting laid again."

"I'm not... *avoiding* him, *per se*...."

Rey wrinkled his nose. "Come on. You broke up with him six months ago."

I sat up straight and felt mildly offended. "Hey, I am over it. I just don't want to see him, which I think is my right as the dumpee in this situation. We never negotiated who got which clubs and coffee houses in the breakup, and I don't want any unpleasant surprises should I go out, you know?"

"Fine." Rey got cut off from speaking when the waitress plunked down plates of food in front of us.

I ate a forkful of pasta. "So. How are things otherwise? If I remember correctly, you are the one who called this Crisis Lunch."

"Eh. Jonny, Uncle Richard. Fucking family. I don't know. If you want to know the truth, Richard has called me three times since I got back from Prague, each time on the pretense of getting me to meet up with Jonathan, but I can't help but think that he's going to make the big announcement soon." He dropped his voice and squared his shoulders. "'I'm Richard Granger and I'm running for president. Even though I'm an old man that the young people don't trust, my nephew Reynolds Blethwyn thinks you should vote for me'." It was a pretty accurate imitation.

"You really think he would do that?" I asked.

"I think he'll want me to endorse him if he's really running for president. And you know that my father will be all over that too."

I nodded, aware that Rey could probably withstand the pressure from his uncle but that he'd cave in the face of pressure from his domineering father. "There's not a whole lot you can do just yet. And you don't even know if Granger is running, so maybe we shouldn't jump the gun. But, um, if your cousin Jonathan wants to meet up, we should invite him out with us sometime."

Rey shrugged noncommittally. "Yeah, I guess I'll have to or I'll never hear the end of it."

"That's the spirit. And I have not seen you in three months. If you have to spend time with Jonny out of familial obligation, I'd rather you bring him along to spend time with me too. Two birds, one stone."

"So you can write your story."

"That is not what I said, but sure. I don't even know if I'm writing the story, though."

Rey sighed. "Okay. I'll call him."

CHAPTER
Three

I WAS in the Laundromat when the announcement was made. As I transferred my laundry from a washer to a dryer, Glynnis, the owner of the Laundromat, turned up the volume on the TV news. "I just love these stupid speeches," she said, settling into a folding chair to watch.

I stopped what I was doing and saw Richard Granger shake hands with a bunch of Republican operatives before taking the podium. He looked like every politician you've ever seen: light-brown hair streaked with gray, ruddy skin, a few extra pounds. He was outside somewhere; there were trees blowing in the background that made for a nice tableau, only I couldn't stand the man who stood in the center of it. The caption at the bottom of the screen indicated that Granger was in Manhattan, Kansas, probably at the university there. He cleared his throat and said, "Good afternoon, everyone." I leaned against the dryer into which I'd just put my clothes and crossed my arms over my chest.

"Good afternoon," Granger repeated. "It's a lovely day, isn't it?" The camera roved over the crowd, which looked like a mix of students and the gray-haired set, who all nodded jovially. Then we were back on Granger. "I'm speaking to you today to announce my candidacy for President of the United States!" The crowd went bonkers, cheering and waving signs. Where the assembled crowd had gotten "Granger for President!" signs was anybody's guess, although I suspected they'd been handed out before the speech, just for this moment. The camera panned back to Granger. He waved his hands, motioning for the crowd to calm down. "If I may say a few words."

And here it came. Glynnis shot me a look, maybe aware of the way I was seething. On screen, Granger said, "Let it be known that I am not just idly running for president. I feel my candidacy is vital, that together we can work hard to restore traditional values to the White House and to the whole country!" He paused to soak up the cheers. Then he changed his face, rendering it serious, looking a little grim, even. "Politicians in Washington have lost sight of what Americans really want. Politics have become angry and divided. We want to unite the people again and work for a better tomorrow!"

The crowd roared. Granger beamed. Then he said, "I plan to run a campaign that upholds our traditional values and morals by looking forward to the future. I want to make an America safe for our children and our children's children." He looked down at the podium, as if he were collecting his thoughts, probably to read whatever other hollow platitudes he'd written in his notes. "I want to stop wasteful spending in Washington. I want to create jobs and lower taxes. I want to defend the traditional values of marriage between one woman and one man and honor the sanctity of life. We at the Granger campaign intend to fight for American values!"

The crowd cheered wildly again, and I felt sick. Glynnis coughed. "Really? The economy's tanking, unemployment's up, and he's running on a values campaign? This guy's a real sleazeball."

"Don't I know it." I considered how tempered the speech was, considering. I'd seen him give a speech a few months before in which he'd talked about—horror of horrors!—a gay couple who had moved into the house down the block from one of his constituents. He'd said publicly that he didn't think gay people had any right being teachers and influencing the minds of children. I doubted the toned-down rhetoric was a reflection of a change of heart so much as his handlers telling him he had to cut out some of the vitriol if he wanted to reach enough moderates to get elected.

On the TV, Granger went on. "A vote for Richard Granger, then, will be a vote for change, a vote for the restoration of the values you hold dear. I will work tirelessly to meet these goals, and I hope you will support me in that. So I, Richard Granger, am running for president. God bless America!"

He took a step away from the podium and smiled at the thunderous applause. Then he gave a little wave to the crowd and the station cut to a reporter.

"God," I said. It was the bit about marriage that was nagging me. I knew why he'd said it, but it galled me that a statement like that had ended up in a speech that should have been about issues like the economy or health care.

Glynnis shook her head. "No way in a million years would a guy like that get elected."

"He got elected to the senate," I pointed out.

"Yeah, in Kansas."

I gave that some thought. "His son lives in New York now. He's related to some powerful famous people too. The right endorsements, a lot of publicity, he could get pretty far. Especially if he's smart and keeps making generic, empty speeches like that one."

Glynnis shook her head. "You are far too cynical, Mr. Walsh. There's no way."

I wasn't so sure.

MY FRIEND Allie was working on Seventeenth Street that fall. I met her for lunch whenever I was in Manhattan. I liked Allie because she was one of the few New Yorkers I knew who didn't have a complex about what she ate; she didn't give a shit about organic or locally grown or even healthy for that matter, and I appreciated her reckless abandon where food was concerned. Maybe this was especially true in contrast to Rey, who had of late taken to eyeing all of his meals suspiciously, as if calories were part of a nefarious conspiracy to make him lose the figure he put many gym hours into maintaining.

Thus Allie and I sat together in Union Square one afternoon, eating soft-serve from a truck and mostly watching people. One of Allie's habits was picking women that were roughly the same size as she was out of a crowd and wondering aloud where they bought their clothes. I licked a great dollop of ice cream from my cone as she finished marveling at a red trench coat that had just walked by.

"I assume you saw the speech yesterday?" she asked after the betrench-coated woman had passed.

"Senator Granger's? Yeah." I was still too angry to really do more than go all *HULK SMASH!* whenever anybody brought his name up, so I was hoping Allie wouldn't want to talk about it too much.

Alas, she said, "He'll never win."

That didn't comfort me in the least. "So everyone keeps telling me, but just the fact that… I mean, there are a lot of people who agree with him. I don't think he's actually *that* radical. So what if he gets elected? Before he started trying to become the leader of the free world, he said some incredibly bigoted things in public. Last year, he gave a speech in which he condemned the repeal of Don't Ask, Don't Tell by calling gay soldiers un-American. He has even been saying that I shouldn't have the right to get married, if, heaven forbid, I should ever find someone willing to put up with me. He was saying I should not exist."

"The tide's changing, Drew. Fewer people believe that."

"I wonder how much of it he even believes," I said, thinking aloud. "It's primary season, after all. The strategy is to inflame the base to motivate them to come out and vote for you, then to back off when it comes to the general election, right? So even if he's talking out of his ass, he's exploiting those in his constituency who *do* believe the things he says. I'm not sure if that's better or worse than if he believed this stuff himself."

"Radicals tend not to get elected."

I appreciated that Allie was trying to talk me down, but I was on a roll now. "What if his son's the same way? I'm supposed to meet him tomorrow night. I don't know how to handle it. I mean, I guess I could tone myself down and hope Rey doesn't say anything, but all it would take is him going through my column archives on the *Forum*'s website, and he'd know not only that I'm a big homo but also that I've more or less built a career on saying bad things about his father and men like him."

Allie rubbed my knee. She smiled in a way that said, "I don't know what to tell you." I gave up and went back to eating my ice cream.

A man ran up the path then. Union Square Park is small enough that it doesn't see a lot of runners, which is probably why this one caught my eye. He was tall and bald with skin the color of dark chocolate, and he was wearing only a pair of tiny running shorts. Sweat glistened all over his muscular body. I couldn't look away. Our eyes met, and he smiled before he continued running. I turned to watch his ass disappear down the path.

"I wonder where he keeps his keys," Allie said.

"I have half a mind to run after him." Normally, I am not a supporter of tiny running shorts, but on this guy, they showcased a fantastic ass. I think I drooled a little.

"Glad your libido works again."

I turned to Allie. "It never stopped working."

"When was the last time you went out, huh? Have you even gone out with anyone since Aaron left?"

"Define 'gone out with'."

She raised an eyebrow. "I'll take that as a no. You have got to get over Aaron."

"Why does everyone keep saying that? I'm not hung up on Aaron."

"You are if you're not dating anyone."

I rolled my eyes. "Maybe I just haven't met anyone."

Allie pointed her ice cream cone at me. "Because you are still hung up on Aaron."

"I just am not eager to set myself up to get my heart stomped on again, okay? Maybe I don't want to be in a relationship right now."

"Who said you had to have a relationship? I saw the look that guy gave you. Wham, bam, thank you, man!"

"I'm a little old for the random hook up, don't you think?" Although, point taken, I acknowledged to myself. I knew well enough that I didn't have to date someone to have sex with him.

Allie sighed. "Fine."

"I have bigger fish to fry anyway. Like Jonathan Granger." And that whole situation was giving me heart palpitations. The more I thought about the story, the more nervous I became.

"It won't be that bad," said Allie. "Maybe it's true that he is gay and he won't have a problem with you."

"You have an awfully simplistic worldview, honey."

Allie groaned. "Look, I don't care. Do what you want. If you want to remain single and miserable for the rest of your life, that's fine with me. You want to obsess about this interview, that's fine too." She looked at me, and I could tell she was trying to look serious and gruff, but a smile won through and she started laughing. I laughed with her. I didn't even know what we were laughing about.

"Life is never easy, is it?" I asked.

CHAPTER
Four

THE second time in my life that I had the premonition that everything was about to change was the moment I first laid eyes on Jonathan Granger.

I was making dinner in Rey's kitchen. Rey was hopeless when it came to cooking, but he had the sort of kitchen that I'd always dreamed of, which seemed unfair. In fact, he lived in the sort of house I had always wanted to own: a gorgeous Park Slope brownstone constructed circa 1890 that had been renovated and restored before he bought it, with five floors and four bedrooms and really much more space than one man needed, but such is the life of a famous actor, I suppose.

Rey leaned on the counter, nursing a beer and making small talk while I cooked. It was pleasant, just the two of us, hanging out like old times. Then the doorbell rang. When Rey went to answer it, all of my nervous nausea came back. I checked on every element of the dinner I was cooking while I waited.

Rey returned, followed by a guy that must have been Jonathan, and, again, I just *knew*. The hair rose on the back of my neck, and I thought, *Oh, fuck*. Rey, oblivious as always, smiled and introduced us.

In an effort not to think about how attractive Jonathan was, I concentrated on looking for family resemblances as we shook hands. They weren't obvious at first. Rey's father and Jonathan's mother were siblings but had chosen very different spouses, so where Rey was all dark good looks inherited from his Dominican mother,

Jonathan looked a little washed out: dirty blond hair, blue eyes, pale skin. And yet they had similar faces: the set of their eyes, the curves of their eyebrows, their long, thin noses. Except where Rey was somewhat broad and boorish at first glance, Jonathan was effete and elegant. He was neatly dressed, not a hair out of place. He had long fingers like a piano player. Where Rey looked strong, Jonathan looked delicate. In other words, Rey was classically movie-star hot. But Jonathan was beautiful.

Rey introduced me as "My old friend Drew."

Jonathan shook my hand. His palm was warm and his handshake firm, which made him seem a little more like a living person and less like porcelain. He smiled warmly. "Nice to meet you," he said.

"Drew is in charge of meal preparation," Rey said. "I don't cook."

"That's a shame," said Jonathan, looking around. "This is a great kitchen."

"My sentiments exactly." I felt the need to talk, to get a word in, to make Jonathan notice me. Like an idiot, I added, "I hope you're not vegetarian, Jonny. There's steak on the menu tonight."

Jonathan turned to me and looked surprised. For the briefest of moments, he looked afraid, but then his face settled into a smile. "Nope," he said. "Steak sounds great."

Our eyes met briefly before his gaze shifted down. I watched his eyes; he looked at my chest for a while, then he abruptly looked up again. I thought maybe he was checking me out, but it was hard to tell if it was that or if he just wanted to know where I bought my shirt. Before I could figure it out, Rey interrupted and said, "Can I get you something to drink? Red wine? Beer?"

"I'd love a beer," Jonathan said.

I faked like I was turning back to my cooking and caught Jonathan looking at me again. I didn't know what to do with that. On the one hand, I was always happy for a man I found attractive to be checking me out. On the other, I really didn't want to be right about my suspicion that he was gay. I'd been hoping that Jonathan would turn out to be the straightest of straight guys so that I could go back to Wade, tell him there was no story, and call it a day. Instinct told me this wasn't meant to be.

Rey escorted him over to the table and told him to sit. They chatted for a moment. I grabbed a short stack of plates and carried them over to the table. "Make yourself useful," I told Rey, handing him the plates. I lingered for a moment, determined now to figure out what was going on in Jonathan's head. He didn't give me any clues. I tried smiling at him, but he frowned and looked at the straw placemat on the table in front of him.

As I walked back to the kitchen, I heard Rey ask, "Is everything okay?"

"What?" said Jonathan. "Yes, everything's fine. This all looks great. Thank you for having me."

I served dinner a little while later, and we all took seats at the table. It took Jonathan a while to warm up enough to drop all the polite posturing, but eventually he did and got to talking. Rey indulged me by asking a few inane questions, and Jonathan turned and explained to me, "I never wanted to go anywhere near politics. So I have a physics degree instead."

"Physics?" I asked, doing what I thought was a decent job of sounding incredulous, even though, of course, I already knew this.

"Yup. I still might go back and get my PhD at some point. I just have the masters so far. The Senator thinks physics was a bizarre form of rebellion, but I love it, really. It's all very logical, unlike politics. I collect old physics textbooks, actually."

"How did you come to teaching, then?" I asked.

Rey shot me a look, eyes narrowed in warning, but Jonathan smiled and said, "I was feeling kind of tired of the aimless academia in college. I read an article saying that inner-city schools were especially hard up for good science teachers, so I got a master's in education, too, then I started applying, and here I am." It was a canned answer, one I would have bet he'd been rehearsing.

"And how's that treating you?" I asked. I leaned forward a little and smiled.

He blushed and dipped his head before answering. "It's good to have something practical to do with my education, but I don't know if I've been at it long enough to reap the rewards, you know?"

It sounded like an honest answer.

"I also have to toe the party line," he added. "Next year's an election year, it's very important that we maintain the image." He spoke with mock self-importance, like he was fully aware of how ridiculous it sounded.

"So is this trip to New York just campaign strategy?" Rey asked.

Jonathan balked and looked at Rey, as if he hadn't realized Rey was there. He looked mildly offended. "No, of course not," he said, shaking his head. "I applied for and got the job here all on my own. But, well, uh. You must have heard by now, Dad just announced he's running for president. It certainly can't hurt if I get a little bit of positive press."

"Seems like a strategy that could backfire badly," I pointed out. I admit, I was egging him on a little. "Your dad does a couple of press conferences with you when he's in New York, shows off his son, but then the camera lenses are all on you, so if you fuck up, everyone notices and you're a liability. And if your father makes it past the primaries, everyone will be all up in his and his family's business. Are you really okay with that?"

Jonathan looked down. "The Bush twins did all right, despite all the negative press early on," he said. "Jenna got a book deal." He plastered a smile on his face, but it wasn't convincing.

"You're not a barely legal pretty blond girl," I said.

Jonathan just shrugged again.

"Not that you don't have certain charms," I added with a grin.

Jonathan looked at me, astonished, but he quickly recovered. "Uh, thanks." He shook his head but smiled, genuinely this time.

Rey grunted softly. "Tell Uncle Richard to leave me out of it."

Jonathan shot Rey a baffled expression. "What would he...?"

Rey sighed. "Sorry, that came out sounding more defensive than I intended. I meant that I have no interest in getting involved in the election race, family or not."

The conversation ceased then, and everyone concentrated on eating. After a while, Jonathan asked, "What do you write about, Drew?"

I wiped my mouth with my napkin before dropping it back in my lap. Jonathan's gaze was on my lips. Yeah, I thought, this was going to be a problem. I was happy enough for the subject change. "Mostly fluff and criticism. I contribute regularly to a couple of small papers, and I write book reviews, that sort of thing."

"Would I have seen your stuff anywhere?"

I glanced at Rey, hoping he'd give me some indication of what I could say. He'd told me it would probably be a bad idea to mention my sexuality in Jonathan's company. He was pretty sure Jonathan didn't share his father's politics, but it had been long enough since they'd seen each other that he didn't know for certain.

"I write a column for the *New York Forum*," I said. When Jonathan looked at me blankly, I let out a breath and added, "It's an alt-weekly. Otherwise, every now and then the *Times* lets me review books for them. And I had a story published in the *New Yorker* a few months ago."

"Wow, really? A story in the *New Yorker*? So are you working on the Great American Novel?"

"Hardly. I'm not a very good fiction writer, I'm much better at biting cultural criticism." I grinned, and Jonathan still looked at me with a blank face. "Well, I did write a screenplay for Rey once, but it's been sitting in a drawer for years."

"That's too bad," said Jonathan.

"Yeah. Do you read much, Jonathan? I just read this really interesting book that I bet you would like. I could lend it to you. It's about...."

While I blabbered, Rey stood and started gathering up the dinner plates now that everyone had finished eating. He looked at me and I decided to ignore him, leaning closer to Jonathan. He was eagerly recounting the plot of the last book he'd finished.

Rey said, "Drew, give me a hand, would you?"

I stood and grabbed a few of the serving dishes. "Can I get you something to drink while I'm up?" I asked Jonathan.

"I'll take another beer."

"Coming right up."

I walked ahead of Rey into the kitchen. I put the dishes in the sink. When I turned around, he was glaring at me. He said, "If you want that interview, you have to back off."

"Back off what?"

"Jonathan."

I shook my head. "What are you talking about?"

"You're *flirting* with him!"

"Oh, I am not. We were just having a nice conversation. Now we can give him a piece of cake and I'll have him sufficiently softened up so that I can swoop in and ask for that interview."

Rey sighed. "And you don't think that he'll be upset that you lied all night?"

"Whoa, I did not lie. He knows I'm a writer and I just told him I write for the *Forum*. And, okay, I feel a little bit bad about not being upfront about my assignment. But I will tell him tonight. He's your cousin and he seems like an okay fellow, so if he says no, I'll go tell Wade Warren to fuck off. Okay?"

Rey rubbed his forehead. "Okay. Fine. I just… I don't want you to do anything that will get him in trouble, you know? Or get you in trouble, for that matter."

"Sure, I get it. And, I mean, I think he's an interesting guy. He's also an adult capable of making his own decisions. Just for the record." I walked over to the fridge and got out two beers.

"Drew, come on. Even if it's true, this is not a situation you should get anywhere near. And I'm not just protecting him."

He didn't need to explain, and honestly, I was touched by his concern, but I breezed past him out of the kitchen anyway.

After we each ate a slice of cake—which I admitted to having purchased at a local bakery; pastry was never my strong suit—the party moved to Rey's first-floor living room. We positioned ourselves on the overstuffed sofas. Rey and Jonathan talked some. I let my body sink into the cushions and thought maybe I'd had a little too much beer with dinner. I didn't feel good about the assignment anymore. I was tempted to forego even mentioning it to Jonathan, but I didn't think I could face Wade again without making at least a halfhearted attempt.

So I tried. "Hey, Jon. Jonny. Uh, do you have a preference?"

"I usually go by Jonathan. I've been trying to phase out Jonny. That's what everyone called me when I was a kid, though, so that hasn't been easy." He leveled his gaze at Rey.

"Okay, Jonathan." God, I even liked how his name rolled off my tongue. I was in deep shit. "I, uh, have a confession to make. And you aren't gonna like it."

Jonathan frowned. I felt for the guy, felt bad about how he was about to get ambushed, but I couldn't think of another way to handle the situation. "Okay," he said.

"I want you to know, now that we've had dinner and gotten to know each other a little bit, I feel absolutely terrible about this."

"God, what is it?" Jonathan asked.

I almost laughed. Something about him was so endearing. His innocence, his obliviousness, something. "I mentioned I write a column for the *Forum*. I also write the occasional feature, usually on things related to my column." And wasn't that the big glittery elephant in the room? I hadn't mentioned anything about the specifics of the columns or even sex generally, having taken Rey's warnings under advisement. Mentioning that I was gay might very well be the end of any relationship, working or otherwise, I had with

Jonathan. I took a deep breath. *Out with it*, I thought. "I got a slightly different assignment last week. Which was to write a feature on you."

Jonathan's eyes widened. "On me?"

"I should have said something sooner. I feel really bad about that."

He didn't look angry, just astonished, his eyebrows raised high. "Why me?"

"Because of who your father is, I guess." I coughed. "You're the son of a senator and you came to New York to teach the disenfranchised youth, so my newspaper thinks you're a person of interest. This is even more true now that your father is officially running for president." I watched the mild horror unfold on Jonathan's. "I'm so sorry. If you want me to go tell my editor where he can stick his story, I will totally do it."

"It's okay," Jonathan said at length. "You're not the first to ask for an interview, and I'm sure you won't be the last. So, what the hell? Let's do it. Write the story on me. I'll make time for an interview. Better to do it with someone I trust, right?"

I laughed. "Yeah, I suppose so. I'd reserve that trust for the time being, though."

"I do trust you."

"You don't know me."

"Well, maybe I'd like to."

Rey cleared his throat. "I'm glad that's settled."

Something rebellious in me wanted to tell Rey he should back off. Instead, I ignored him. "Thanks," I said to Jonathan. "I really appreciate it. We could get together, drinks or dinner or something, later this week? Something casual." And in a public place, I almost added. "Would that be all right?"

"Yeah," said Jonathan. "I think that would be fine. Or do you want to come by the school this week? You could see my classroom."

We made arrangements. Before long, Jonathan yawned and said he should probably get going before he passed out on the couch. He went back to the formal politeness, shook each of our hands, and then left.

I stayed in the living room while Rey walked him out. When Rey came back, he said, "Well, that was not an *unmitigated* disaster. But, see, he's more interested in talking about teaching than politics. And I still think he's straight. So there may be no story here at all."

I sighed. I didn't feel up to sharing my suspicions with Rey. "Yeah," was all I said.

CHAPTER
Five

I PUT on a suit for my interview with Jonathan. Kind of. I had never been good at formal dressing, so I left off the tie and decided to leave the shirt untucked. That way, I reasoned, I looked somewhat professional, but it didn't look like I was trying too hard.

I met him at Brooklyn Technical High School. Though it was public, it was among the city's elite magnet schools and required an entrance exam to get in. Kids from all over the city attended, and they tended to be among the cleverer of their peers. This was why, even though he was teaching in Brooklyn, I thought Jonathan had gotten a pretty plum assignment. Teaching honors kids at Brooklyn Tech was a far cry from teaching at a zone school in a rougher neighborhood.

We'd made arrangements for me to observe his last class of the day. I got to the school a few minutes early, dealt with security, and then found Jonathan's classroom. When the bell rang, I walked into the room against the tide of students rushing out. Jonathan spotted me right away—at six foot four I do sometimes stick out in a crowd—and gave me what looked like a tired smile.

"Hi," I said when I got to his desk. "I hope this is still all right. I'll stay out of your way, I promise."

He looked me over. Then he blushed and turned away, gesturing towards the back of the classroom. "That desk in the back left corner is unassigned, if you want to sit there."

I hadn't been inside a classroom since I'd graduated from college. This was all very disconcerting and familiar. "Yeah, okay. Been a while since I had to sit at a school desk."

"I'd let you sit up here," Jonathan said, gesturing towards his own chair, "but I don't want the kids to get distracted by you."

"Out of sight, out of mind." I winked to show I understood. I walked over to the back corner and took the seat. I realized—and judging by the look on his face, Jonathan made the same realization at the same time—that though the kids probably wouldn't see me, this meant we'd be in sight of each other for the next forty minutes.

The class wandered in. Jonathan—Mr. Granger to the kids—introduced me to the class, then launched into his lecture. Given how shy he'd been when we'd first met, I was surprised to learn he was a charismatic speaker. I'd sort of skated through my high school science classes, taking the minimum of what I needed to get into college and even then getting mostly C's. I wondered idly if having a teacher like Jonathan would have made a difference. He had a way of explaining things that made sense without treating his students like they were idiots. He cracked jokes and good-naturedly answered his students' questions.

Then again, he was so cute that, if I had been a student in his class, I probably would have spent most of the period staring at him all moony-eyed and wouldn't have heard a word he said. He looked cute, in kind of a preppy way, wearing a button-down-and-tie combo, and he had a bashful grin. I pictured myself as a student in his class and imagined I'd doodle his name on my binder and mentally plan our wedding. Hell, I was kind of doing that anyway.

The kids filed out when the bell rang, and I walked back up to the front of the classroom. "Wow. You're good. I bet I could pass the Regents exam now," I said, referring to the test required for all New York high school students.

"Right," said Jonathan with an eye-roll, though he smiled.

"Well, I think it's safe to say that anyone who doubts your qualifications to teach can kiss my ass, because you're definitely a good teacher, not just here because of your father." I winced when I realized how thick I was laying it on.

He didn't seem to notice. "Thank you. I appreciate that."

"That was your last class, right? Do you have time to talk now? If not here, there's a coffee shop on Myrtle I like."

"Okay. Yeah. We should go to the coffee shop. Let me just get some things together."

After Jonathan shoved a bunch of papers in his bag, we made our way out of the school and he followed me up to Myrtle Avenue. "I live in the neighborhood," I explained. "Six or seven blocks over that way." I pointed vaguely in the direction of my apartment.

"Cool," he said. Then he laughed. "I know how to get from the subway to the school, and that's kind of it. You could have just pointed anywhere. I know almost nothing about the neighborhood. You like it here?"

"Yeah, I do. I think it's a good mix of students and young families. Lots of new businesses too. All these great little restaurants and shops have opened in the six or so years I've been here."

We got to the café, and I bought us each a coffee before settling down at a table in the corner. I pulled out a notebook and a tape recorder from the backpack I'd been carrying. "So," I said. "You don't mind if I record this, do you?"

"No, it's okay."

I looked at the tape recorder and wondered how best to handle this. "We should have a safe word or something. If you get uncomfortable, if you say something you don't want to be public knowledge, you'll have to let me know."

"Deal," Jonathan said, though he was already looking uncomfortable. "Safe word?"

"You know, something you say if you start panicking and the situation doesn't sit well anymore. If I start flogging you too hard, so to speak."

He giggled. "Um, okay."

"Just, uh, if I say something or ask you a question you're uncomfortable with, say, uh...." I looked around the room. One wall had mural of tropical fruit painted on it. I said the first thing that popped into my head: "Pineapple."

The first batch of questions was all routine, mostly stuff he'd already talked about publicly or with me. Where he went to college, why he chose teaching, why he came to New York. He talked a little about his frustration with not landing a more difficult job, which I thought was interesting. "I did my student teaching at this under-funded school in DC. I learned a lot there. When I started applying for jobs at inner-city schools, I thought, 'I really want to help these kids.' Kids with few resources, I mean. And I did some volunteer work and college fairs and that sort of thing. But then someone up here caught wind of who my father was, and I got offered this job at Brooklyn Tech. Not to sound ungrateful, but Tech is one of the best high schools in the city. For the most part, my students are overachievers, the sorts of kids who are definitely going somewhere. They just need me to teach them this stuff and give them a good grade, they don't really need my *help*, you know?"

"Be careful what you wish for. A college friend of mine was a teaching fellow in the city. She joined this local program where they stick you in a classroom and pay for your masters. You may not think so, but believe me when I tell you that you're probably better off, especially if you're new here. She grew up in Brooklyn and teaching in Bed-Stuy still almost broke her. Get a couple of years teaching under your belt, then you can go be the guy from *Stand and Deliver*."

He nodded and seemed to consider my advice. Everything continued to go well, the conversation flowed easily, but I knew it was going to have to get more difficult.

I couldn't decide if I should ask him directly about Wade's rumor or if I should even hint at it. The real nature of the assignment sat in the back of my mind. I turned over a dozen ways to approach the situation in my mind. Ultimately, I said, "So, we need to get into some meatier things to keep the article interesting. If you want to know the truth, I think the main reason I was chosen to write this story, even though it's not my usual thing, is that I've written some really scathing things about your father."

There was a pause before Jonathan said, "Who hasn't?"

"Ha. Right. Well, I mean, I think my editor was thinking that I, as a vocal critic of Senator Granger, could lend something interesting to a story about his son."

"Dad is the senator from Kansas. Why would a columnist in New York take much interest in him?" I thought he was feigning more than actually being innocent.

"He's spearheaded some legislature I opposed," I said, playing along.

"Oh."

"Maybe we should talk about politics, then. Just, uh, how eye-to-eye are you and your father?"

Jonathan hesitated. "He's my father. I support him."

Standard party line, of course. That was disappointing. "Of course."

He laughed and shook his head. "I mean, I support my father. I don't always agree with him."

"On what kinds of things do you disagree?"

"I…." He hesitated again. "Mostly, uh… you know, I don't really want to be involved in politics, like I told you a few days ago. I try to stay out of it."

"Surely you have some opinions, though."

"Well, yeah, but—"

And then I launched right in there. "Gay rights, for example. Your father has come out in favor of the Defense of Marriage Act, he opposed the repeal of Don't Ask, Don't Tell, and he's said publicly that gay men are 'deviants' who shouldn't be teaching in schools or attending churches."

Jonathan shook his head. "I don't think all gay men are deviants."

I couldn't stop myself. I raised an eyebrow. "Not all? So some of them?"

He got a little flustered. "No, I mean... look, I'm not really comfortable publicly disagreeing with my father."

"So give me a statement I can print."

Jonathan leaned back and took a sip of his coffee. "He's running on a campaign of 'traditional American values', which means an emphasis on, what, family? Supporting the country? That's a good stance, right?"

"So you're saying you support your father's positions on social policy?"

"No, I...." Jonathan frowned. "He's my father, I support him. I don't always agree with him, though. Off the record? I think government has no business meddling in people's personal lives. We all have the right to do and think and say as we please, within the parameters of the law. My father wants to regulate behavior, but...."

When Jonathan stopped talking, I waited, doodling on my notepad. After a long pause, I prodded, "But...?"

"But you can't regulate behavior. I mean, government exists to keep people from destroying each other, right? So there are laws against murder and mistreating children, but you can't... you can't regulate people's essential natures."

I needed him to say it. Part of me wanted him to just blurt, "I'm gay!" so we wouldn't have to keep dancing around this. Fat chance. "So what are you saying?"

"The Senator thinks that stripping gays of their rights will make them go away. He figures if he denies a gay man his rights, that gay man will choose not to be gay anymore. But even I know that's not how it works. That is, I...." He looked down at the table. "I want you to know that I don't think he's right, about gay people being stripped of their rights I mean. But I don't know if I can say that in a public forum."

"So you're telling me, but you don't want it printed."

"Yeah."

"Why would you want me to know?"

Jonathan squirmed in his seat. "I guess I didn't want you to think that I was like him, that I thought that way."

I hit the stop button on the recorder and said, "Look, there's probably something else you should know."

Jonathan bit his lip. "Okay."

"In the interest of full disclosure, I brought you a copy of the *Forum* with my column in it."

Yes, that was how I decided to come out to him. It was cowardly, I know, but telling my extended family had not been this difficult. Not only was I afraid of any repercussions as pertained to his cooperation with the article, but I was starting to really like him. I recognized that nothing would ever come of any of this if I was too chicken to tell him I was gay and Jonathan was too straight or closeted to return my affections, and that if he were indeed put off by my orientation, I didn't need him anyway, but still, I didn't want to alienate him or piss him off. I wasn't ready to push him away quite yet. Did I mention the long fingers and the pretty eyes and my complete surprise that he was so down to earth?

Jonathan took the paper I offered and flipped through it.

And on went my tongue: "The *Forum*'s not exactly the *Times*, you know? I mean, it's supposed to be this sort of underground thing. We mostly cover goings-on in the city, pop culture, that kind of thing. The paper has a decidedly lefty bent."

"Which you think I'd be offended by because of who my father is?"

"Yeah, maybe."

He didn't respond. He continued to flip until he stopped suddenly, his eyes wide. He'd found my column, presumably. I watched him read for a minute. I'd deliberately chosen a somewhat innocuous column, one that was mostly a review of this ridiculous indie movie that its producers thought was supposed to be the next *Brokeback Mountain* in terms of bringing the problems of the gays to the masses, but the whole thing was a corny schlockfest, in my humble opinion. In the column, I occasionally referred to "the gay community" and its reaction to the film as "we" and "our." I was hoping Jonathan would read between the lines.

"I just thought you should know what you're in for," I said. "This kind of fluffy, positive feature story is not my usual deal."

"Why did your editor assign you this job, then?" He might as well have asked me outright if I was gay, as naked as his gaze and the question made me feel.

"I wasn't sure, either, but then I thought that maybe you could shed some light on that." This was a stab in the dark. I couldn't tell if he was being deliberately obtuse or if he was really that oblivious. Either way, he wasn't going to just volunteer the information I needed from him.

"How would I know what your editor was thinking?"

I sighed and turned the recorder back on. I thought of every action hero who ever said "I'm gonna go for broke" before hurling himself into a dangerous situation. Only, you know, I wouldn't have wanted any harm to come to my Hugo Boss suit, so I didn't hurl myself so much as take a heavy step forward. "Time for some indelicate questions about your personal life."

Jonathan had been slowly working up to a good panic since the moment I handed him the newspaper. You could see it all over his face when I brought up his personal life, in the way his eyes darted around, the tiny beads of sweat on his forehead. He wouldn't look at me. "Okay," he said shakily.

"I mean, the *Forum*'s readers want a little bit of dirt. You seeing anybody? Got a girl waiting for you back in DC?"

"No. There's no dirt on me." His voice cracked as he spoke, though, and he winced. "Pineapple."

Bingo, I thought. Jonathan's shame was suddenly palpable, his face red as he sank into his chair a little, his brow furrowed. He looked completely miserable. I nodded. "Fair enough. I'm not here to make you uncomfortable. There's something you don't want people to know, don't tell me. You said you trust me. I'd prefer not to betray that."

"Thank you."

"I mean, I like you, Jonathan. You seem like a good guy."

"I like to think I am."

I turned the recorder back off again. "This is not what I expected. For the most part, I'm pleasantly surprised. I'll admit, I feared the worst. And I wish you would let me print some of this stuff about you and your father. Disagreement is interesting. You saying something to refute some of Senator Granger's rhetoric, some of what he's said in his speeches, that would make for a good story." He didn't really acknowledge me, just stared unfocused at the table between us. "Okay, I guess I have enough to write a story. It'll be safe, but it's what my editor asked for."

"I'm sorry, but I just can't—"

Then, because I couldn't help myself, I added, "I wonder if your father has some kind of personal vendetta. I mean, has he even met a gay person? Does he know the effect his words have on people?"

Jonathan rubbed his forehead. "I can't really answer that."

So there would be no confession, but after all that, I had no doubt in my mind that Jonathan Granger was indeed gay and very deeply in the closet. Which was when I decided to drop it. "Well. You should probably be prepared for more press after the story hits the newsstands. And, assuming I get my shit together in a timely fashion, the story will probably be in next week's paper. My editor is putting some pressure on me to hurry and get it done as soon as possible to time it with the Senator's announcement."

"Of course."

I started putting my various paraphernalia back in my backpack. "Thanks, Jonathan. I'm glad you sat down to talk to me."

He didn't look so glad. But then, when I reached for my notebook, Jonathan grabbed it. He hastily scribbled a phone number on the open page. "You can call me. If you have more questions, I mean."

I looked at him for a long time, trying to get a bead on his intentions. "If I have more questions. Sure."

Jonathan tossed our coffee cups in the trash, then moved toward the door. He asked me for directions back to the subway, and I pointed him towards it. As he moved to walk away, I stood on the sidewalk, wanting that confession, not for the article but for me. But I couldn't bring myself to ask the question. Instead, I said, "Look for the story next week."

"Thanks," he said. I watched him walk back to the subway.

CHAPTER
Six

REY and I did not see eye to eye on interior decorating, which was something I got an earful about during a brief interlude when Rey was having the top floor of his house re-done. I decided to let him stay with me, meaning he slummed it by camping out on the futon in my living room. It was a mod furniture special with a lime-green cover on the mattress. I liked things that were clean and modern and brightly colored. Rey's house was more muted and decorated in what I thought of as "pricey cheap," furniture he paid full price for at high-end shops but that looked like it could have been bought at a thrift store.

Anyway, he'd told me on many occasions that he thought my futon couch was maybe the ugliest thing he'd ever set eyes on, so I was somewhat surprised to find him asleep on it when I came in one afternoon. He'd kept his keys from when he'd stayed with me in case of emergency, which usually meant that he just let himself in if he was coming to see me instead of knocking like a normal person.

I stood over him for a moment, and he slowly opened his eyes. I said, "Don't you have those overstuffed monstrosities in your own house for use at nap time?"

Rey rubbed his eyes and sat up. "Oh, sure," he said, "but I thought what I really needed was an unsatisfying nap and some back pain. What the hell is this stuffed with, Styrofoam?"

"To what do I owe this pleasure?"

"I wanted your advice on something."

I sat and draped an arm over the back of the futon. I flicked at an errant lock of Rey's hair with the tip of my finger. "Don't do it," I said.

"You don't even know what I'm going to ask yet."

"No, but I recognize that expression on your face. That's the look you get when you're going to ask my opinion on something but already know I won't approve. I'm saving us time, see."

"You and the high horse. I don't know where you get off judging me, like you're so righteous. You're so afraid of anything bad happening that you don't ever take any risks anymore."

I tried not to get too defensive, primarily because I didn't want him to know that he was kind of right. "I take risks," I said.

"No, you don't. I talked to Allie. She said you hardly ever go out anymore because you're still avoiding Aaron."

Geez Louise, why was everyone so obsessed with this? "I'm not avoiding Aaron."

"If you're not going to the places where you and Aaron used to hang out because you're afraid of running into him, you're avoiding Aaron."

"I prefer to think of it as giving us both space."

"So it's true."

I shrugged. Okay, so *maybe* I was avoiding Aaron. But there were armed conflicts that had more peaceful resolutions than our relationship. I deserved some slack. I tried to sound casual. "Maybe. It's probably better for my soul if I spend less time in gay bars. I'm not a twenty-two-year-old twink anymore."

Rey pursed his lips, looking skeptical.

"Look, I know that what happened is for the best, but Aaron and I were together for more than a year, so I think I deserve a little bit of time to mourn. But you did not come here to pester me about Aaron. Stop stalling. What do you need advice about?"

Rey rolled his eyes. "I need a date for the show's premiere."

I put a hand on his chest and batted my eyelashes. "And you're asking me? Honey, I'm flattered."

"No, you idiot. A female date."

"I think I could pull off looking like a woman. I have a very pretty face. The right wig, a stuffed bra. What do you think?"

Rey laughed. I preened.

"If you were a foot shorter, maybe," he said. "I hate to do this to you, man, but I'm not bringing you to the premiere."

"Boo."

"What do you think of me asking Allie?"

That was not something I liked one bit. "Aren't there any aspiring starlets whose hearts you can break? The last time you went out with one of my friends, she stopped talking to me."

"She moved to Virginia for a job."

"Still. I like Allie. I want to keep her. She has a little bit of a crush on you as it is. You know I love you, but you, my friend, have a terrible track record with women. You going out with her... that can only end badly."

"Fine. Maybe I'll ask one of my costars."

"Good."

There was a pause. "How'd the interview with Jonathan go?"

"It went okay. I'm not allowed to print anything good, but it went okay."

"What do you mean, you aren't allowed to print anything good?"

I shifted on the couch. "I got him to tell me that he disagrees with his father on social issues, specifically on that whole banning-gays-from-the-country thing, but he told me he doesn't want to get caught publicly disagreeing with the Senator. He just wanted *me* to know."

"Right. Did you tell him you're gay?"

"Not in so many words."

Rey raised his eyebrows. "What does that mean?"

"I showed him one of my *Forum* columns, but I didn't say anything else on the matter. Not that it's a big secret, of course."

He sighed. "Probably he put together that the *Forum* is lefty propaganda and didn't want to piss you off. Or he read your column and figured you are not in favor of Uncle Richard's stance on stripping you of more of your rights."

"Or he wants something else." I raised an eyebrow. I hadn't let myself entertain the possibility that he could possibly want *me*, but there it was.

Rey understood. "Wishful thinking."

"On whose part?"

He rolled his eyes. "I still think you're wrong about Jonathan. He's not gay. I'd know."

"You didn't know I'm gay until I told you. Actually, I don't think you *really* knew until you walked in on me having sex with Jake Monaghan back when we roomed together."

Rey winced. "We were young. I didn't know anything back then."

"Well, anyway, I'm writing a really tame article and Wade's going to hate it. So I must somehow reconcile the fact that your cousin came off as nice and sweet but kind of boring with the fact that if I don't turn in an interesting story, Wade will never hire me for a feature story again."

"There isn't always a story."

I stood to motion Rey out of the apartment. "That's not the problem here. The problem is that there *is* a story here, but Jonathan won't let me tell it."

I HESITATED, my phone in my hand, my thumb hovering over the "send" button. I worried I'd misinterpreted the situation, but then,

Jonathan had given me his phone number. He wouldn't have done that if he hadn't wanted me to call, I told myself.

I am not always the best judge of people's behavior. I once spent a good twenty minutes flirting with a guy at a bar, thinking he was really into it, only to have him tell me he and his *partner* were both big fans of my column. But there had been something in Jonathan's eyes when he looked at me, some understanding and, I was pretty sure, attraction. But I still hesitated. I had spent the better part of the last few days steeped in Jonathan Granger lore, digging up background information for the article and looking for confirmation of Wade's source's information. I'd found a couple of stories in the Georgetown student paper that mentioned him, but I hadn't unearthed anything revealing. I wondered if Wade even had a source or if it was all made up.

Still, there was that phone number scribbled in my notebook, and the story was hitting newsstands that Monday anyway, so I felt fairly confident in calling up Jonathan to invite him to dinner. Just dinner, at first, to celebrate the article's publication, and if the hot sex I imagined we would have came too, that was a bonus. (Rey had called that correctly. I am the king of wishful thinking.) If I was reading the signs wrong and Jonathan wasn't interested in anything more than friendship, well, it still wouldn't be too embarrassing if I called. Just dinner. Platonic friends had dinner.

I hit "send." Jonathan answered on the third ring.

"Hi, Jonathan? It's Drew Walsh."

"Hello."

The flat reaction gave me pause. "Uh. I was just calling because… well, the article is going to be in Monday's paper, and I thought maybe, if you're not doing anything later this week, we could get a bite to eat and celebrate?"

There was a pause so long that I had to pull the phone away from my ear to verify the call was still connected. Eventually, he said, "Um. Like a date?"

Wow. Having never been a straight man, I wasn't certain, but I felt pretty confident that the first assumption of one being asked to dinner by another man was not that they were going on a date. At the mild horror in Jonathan's tone, I said, "No, no, just dinner. A celebration for the article. You know, food, wine, maybe a slice of chocolate cake at the end. Just dinner."

"All right. If it's a celebration. I can do just dinner. How's Wednesday?"

WADE WARREN was disappointed with the article's lack of dirt. I explained that, even after a few well-placed calls at Georgetown, I hadn't come up with any confirmation of the source's information—I did not relate my own suspicions to Wade—so I didn't feel comfortable writing anything about Jonathan's personal life lest Senator Granger's camp decided to sue the crap out of the paper. The potential for a lawsuit convinced Wade to acquiesce. He made a few changes to what had been a fairly straightforward profile, because, all things considered, *Forum* readers probably didn't really give a shit about Jonathan Granger. Thus, more of my history as a critic of Richard Granger had been added to the story. Wade told me it added some pop.

Thinking it only fair to warn Jonathan, I called him Sunday night. Well, that, and I wanted to talk to him again. Just because. "I think I've learned a valuable lesson," I told him when he answered the phone.

He laughed. "What's that?"

"From now on, I will only tell you the whole truth, okay? Because I am, once again, calling to tell you something I should have told you two weeks ago."

"What is it?" he asked, sounding a little worried.

"I know you weren't happy with the discussion of politics in the interview, but I needed something to give the story some interest, so there's some stuff in the article both about the way that I, personally, have criticized your father and about how you had some reservations about some of his positions. I tried to be reasonable because I know you want to respect your father, but there's some stuff in the story. I've written about Senator Granger extensively in the past, and I've said some nasty things."

"Thanks for the warning." There was a long pause, and then he said, "Um. Are we still on for Wednesday?"

I let out a sigh of relief. "Sure, if you don't hate me after the article is published."

"People say mean things about my father all the time. It's part of the bargain when one is a part of public life. He supports things you disagree with. You said yourself that you work for a paper with a liberal bent. I get it, I do. No offense taken."

"Hold that thought until you see the article."

"Drew."

"If you don't want to murder me, I'll see you on Wednesday."

I couldn't quite shake my guilt, because the truth was I liked Jonathan, more than was appropriate, and I didn't want to alienate the man. I'd worried when I'd handed in the story that the stupid crush I was developing had compromised it, but Wade hadn't seemed to notice. So that was something, at least.

The real fear, though, was that Jonathan would like the story and then delve into the *Forum*'s archives. Part of me worried that if Jonathan knew the real reason I had directed so much vitriol towards his father, it would send him running away screaming.

THE story did, indeed, hit newsstands Monday morning. Not my finest work, I will admit. It was kind of a gushy piece, or the first draft had been. When I picked up the paper, I saw Wade had re-tooled a lot of the first few paragraphs.

The story opened, "Longtime readers know I'm no fan of Senator Richard Granger from Kansas. Over the years, I've called him everything from a bigoted blowhard to the greatest evil ever visited on the country. (I may have used a tad bit of hyperbole in that column). His continued support of anti-gay legislation—including the Defense of Marriage Act, not to mention that roaring speech he gave when he announced his candidacy for president—on the grounds that gay people are unnatural, a pox on society, or, at minimum, undeserving of basic civil rights particularly pisses me off, for obvious reasons. I was therefore surprised to like his son so much."

The subtext was, of course, "Dear Jonathan, I'm gay, please go out with me," but I thought it was appropriately subtle. I don't know why I was so reluctant to just tell him I was gay. If he did get scared off, well, it wasn't like he would have slept with me anyway.

The article itself was a complimentary portrait of Jonathan, focusing on his teaching goals and what he was doing in the classroom. I'd put a paragraph in the middle of the article about how he didn't always see eye to eye with his father, but it was vague and I'd spun it as Jonathan being his own man, a smart man able to think for himself.

So all in all, I thought it was a success. I hoped Jonathan agreed.

CHAPTER
Seven

ONE of the things that I admired about Rey was that, messy love life and big fancy house notwithstanding, he continued to be his old modest self, even after he started getting recognized on the street. He and I were out to lunch one time when a woman walked to our table and nearly fell over herself gushing. He'd talked to her like she was a calm, intelligent woman, he'd autographed a napkin for her, and then he'd gone back to having lunch with me like it was nothing. Maybe it was. Even when I saw him on TV, I had a hard time seeing him as Reynolds Blethwyn. To me, he was still the guy whose clothes I borrowed as a teenager, whom I used to get into epic water-gun fights with on hot summer days, who skinned his knee that time I thought it would be a good idea to rollerblade through the hilliest part of the town park. He was still my friend Rey, who slept on my couch when his house was being remodeled, who listened to my relationship problems, who came to me for advice.

And, sure, I'd had a crush on him in high school, but he'd become my brother. He had a much older sister whom he wasn't close to, so I think he thought of himself as an only child also. Or maybe he was the odd one out a lot at home. His sister and her husband had gone into the family business, both of them working at Rey's father's paper plant. His sister was being groomed to take over the company. I knew that Rey's father had seen his early aptitude for math and decided it was his destiny to become a businessman too, but that was not what Rey wanted.

Being the one who didn't belong, that was something I understood. I figured we'd always not belong together.

Maybe that made Rey's success all the more surreal. The longer his tenure on the show, the more his skills were touted in the media, the more he became a part of this pop culture machine. It was like being the most popular kid in school but, like, on steroids. I wondered sometimes if he'd leave me behind. Most of the time, I knew in my heart that he needed me as much as I needed him, but fame and fortune were hard things to compete with.

MY DINNER with Jonathan coincided with the premiere of the newest season of Rey's TV show. *Brooklyn Heights* was an evening soap, sort of a *Melrose Place* set in New York. In the second season, Rey had been cast to play the love interest of one of the leads, and he'd become something of a fan favorite. They'd added his name to the credits in the third season, which to me made it seem like he was impossibly famous.

I walked into the restaurant where Jonathan and I had arranged to meet. He'd beat me there and was already seated at a table. He looked good. His hair had too much gel in it, and he had a misguided affinity for polo shirts, but these were transgressions for which I could forgive him. I had opted for a white button-down shirt and jeans; the look I was going for was "Oh, this old thing" and not the result of what had really transpired, which was that I'd changed clothes at least five times before I'd left my apartment, trying to find the perfect outfit, the thing that would make Jonathan want me.

I think I was successful. His gaze lingered on my chest as I sat down across from him.

"How was your day?" I asked him as I picked up a menu.

"All right. Busy."

"Good, good. I'm, ah, glad you showed up."

"Were you worried I wouldn't?"

I had been, yes. I pretended to look at the menu. This was a slightly pretentious French bistro near Union Square. I don't know why I picked it. The food was decent and they had a good wine list, but now that I looked at the be-polo-shirted object of my affection, I wondered if it wasn't too upscale a choice.

I said, "By the way, the premiere of *Brooklyn Heights* is tonight at nine, and I want to be home for that. Or at least near a TV. You're welcome to join me."

Jonathan bit his lip. "Are you inviting me to your place after dinner?" His voice was strained, like he was also putting up the same tense, faux-casual façade that I was giving him. For some reason, that helped me calm down.

"Not necessarily," I said. "I'm just saying that my best friend's TV show is on at nine and I'd like to watch it. If you are interested in seeing it too but don't feel up to going to my place, I know a bar in the East Village that puts it on every week."

The waiter came by and we ordered drinks. I had a glass of a sauvignon blanc that I knew was good; Jonathan ordered a scotch neat.

"Do you always watch Rey?" Jonathan asked after the waiter left again.

I knew it was a loaded question. I think what he really wanted to know was if I had feelings for his cousin. I hated that we were playing this game, but I didn't know how to get beyond that without opening a can of worms. "Yeah, when I can. Have you seen the show?"

"No. Well, I saw Rey's first episode. My family threw a party and made a big deal out of it. I found it very strange to see someone I'd known my whole life on the TV, you know? It freaked me out a little. I never got around to watching another episode after that."

I could relate. Rey had been in all the school plays, and that was one thing, but the first time I saw him on TV—he'd played a witness on an episode of *Law & Order*—I'd laughed so hard I missed his one line. I think that was also the one time he'd actually played a Latino character. He hadn't made much of a secret of his half-Dominican ancestry in interviews, and he'd even been nominated for an American Latino Media Arts Award after his first season on *Brooklyn Heights*, but if you didn't know better, you'd guess he was Italian or Greek, with his dark hair, olive skin, and startling blue eyes.

But enough about Rey. To Jonathan, I said, "Well, I was a fan of the show before Rey got cast on it, so that was exciting. Before that, he did mostly bit parts and walk-on roles. But he did manage to get himself cast in theater periodically, and I've been to every play. I wanted to be supportive, but not all of it's been good. He did a lot of avant-garde theater right after college. There was one play where the entirety of his role entailed riding a stationary bike while wearing only green body paint and a thong."

"Uh...."

I laughed. "Don't ask me to explain. I don't think I could if I had to. I'm sure it had deep significance."

Jonathan smiled. He had a great smile, charming and boyish. I wanted to kiss it right off his face. Man, I was in trouble. He said, "Yeah, I had a friend in college who was an artist. She did really crazy sculpture. Would pin Barbie doll parts to cork boards and call it something like 'The Failure of the American Dream'."

That made me chuckle. I think I knew the same girl in college. "There's a point at which it becomes so obscure it just loses its meaning. Like Dada, but even more pretentious."

Drinks appeared and Jonathan took a healthy sip of his scotch.

"For what it's worth," he said after a moment, "I liked the article. I mean, there were the digs at Dad and the mention of our disagreements, but I'm really flattered, actually. A few people at school have come up to me to talk about it, and I think I've even gained some of their respect." He sighed. "This is going to come across as sounding whiney and ungrateful, but it's been tough, these first few weeks at the job. I just wanted to teach, but the Senator arranged for the freakin' mayor to come down to the school on my first day, and ever since then, I think most of my colleagues assumed I got the job because of who my father is. But you said some really nice things about my teaching in the article, and I think maybe you changed a few minds. I'm really thankful for that. And now I feel like a minor celebrity." His smile was a little wistful.

"Well, that's good." I didn't know what to say. I took a sip of my wine and let it sit on my tongue for a moment. I was nervous again and hardly tasted it. "You never got attention like that before? Not even in Washington? I imagine plenty of people knew who you were, or knew who your father was. No one ever came up to you in a cafe to ask for a favor from your father?"

Jonathan shrugged. "I've always kind of flown under the radar. I mean, yeah, my father is an important man, but who am I? I don't matter." He looked down at his glass. I saw it was empty. That was fast. He signaled the waiter.

Feeling a little daring, I said, "I think you matter."

"You barely know me."

"I'd like to know you."

Jonathan sighed heavily. "Maybe this was a mistake."

"Just dinner," I reminded him. "Unless there's something else going on here?"

"I don't know what you're talking about." He said it like someone who knew exactly what I was talking about.

"I think you do." Apparently having reached my threshold for putting up with bullshit, I said, "I think you're maybe more grateful for what I didn't put in that article than for what I did."

Jonathan looked down.

A new round of drinks appeared. Jonathan gulped down more scotch before he looked at me. Our eyes met. His eyes were amazing, shining green in the light of the restaurant.

"I can't," he said in response to the unasked question. "I'm not."

"Fine," I said.

He looked around the room. I followed his gaze towards a table full of women. All five of them were beautiful; there was no denying that. Jonathan looked wistful. When he looked back at me, his face was totally naked. There was just something in his eyes, some old pain that I recognized. I could see it all there, emotions I was familiar with reflected back at me, and I knew he'd been struggling for years to cope with this and hadn't found a way to yet.

He said, "You aren't... anything I say is confidential, right?"

I found that insulting. "You mean, am I recording you? Am I going to turn around and write a story about this? Come on, Jonathan. I invited you to dinner, not to ambush you. I hope you would think more of me by now."

"I do. I trust you. The article was good. If you had any idea about... well, you didn't mention it, and I *am* grateful." He looked down. I think he realized he'd just confirmed it. "I'm sorry. I didn't mean to doubt you. But there's no way you could understand."

I scoffed. Under my breath, I said, "Could understand what? What it's like to be gay? I have an inkling."

He shook his head. "It's not just that."

"Then tell me what it is."

He contemplated the glass in his hand for a long moment. At length, he said, "I'm the end of the line, you know that?"

"What?"

He sighed. "I'm my only-child father's only son. Six generations of Grangers in this country, and I'm it."

I couldn't process what he was getting at. "So?"

"I'm trying to explain. There's a legacy to be concerned with, just to begin with. And you know who my father is, you know what he stands for, maybe better than anyone. I haven't had time to read the archives of your column, but one of my colleagues gave me a rundown of the things you've written about the Senator. A lot of it's angry, right?"

I grunted.

"See, now you're getting the wrong idea. I was actually glad you called me, and I came to dinner willingly. Against my better judgment, I like you a lot. I admit, I was sort of hoping that this would be a little bit more than just a celebration dinner for the article."

"But?"

"As a friend, I like you as a friend. That's all this can be."

Man, I was getting dumped before I even got to have sex with the guy. I took a sip of my wine. I thought this dinner was maybe on its way toward an end, that Jonathan would get up and leave and that would be the end of this whole interlude in my life.

Except then he said, "Lesbians are trendy."

And I laughed. "Geez, you and the non-sequiturs."

"What I mean is it's trendy for politicians to have gay female family members. Newt Gingrich's sister, Dick Cheney's daughter. Lesbians are to be condemned by conservative politicians in public, but they are ultimately non-threatening. They're still women. They get married and have babies. And it's okay to be a conservative politician and have a lesbian daughter. Gay men are still too scary, too threatening to most conservatives' macho sense of masculinity. It is not okay to have a gay son. Do you see what I'm saying?"

I stared at him with some measure of disbelief before I said, "So you would deny a part of yourself for the sake of your father's image? Just excise it like a tumor?"

"I'm not gay."

"Right. And I don't have brown hair."

He glanced up at my hair, which, for the record, is indeed very brown. "I'm not," he repeated. "I can't be. It's not an option."

"Well. That sucks, then."

"I've been with plenty of women," he said, as if that settled it.

"I'm sure you have. That doesn't prove anything."

"I love my father."

"Maybe you do. I bet you don't like him much."

Jonathan didn't say anything. I guessed he couldn't deny that.

I said, "Don't take this personally, but he's one of the few politicians outside of the New York metropolitan area that I pay attention to, and it's mostly because what he stands for is so offensive. He talks all the time about marriage being only for hetero couples. He mentioned it again when he made the big announcement. Then he voted for that bill that would deny gay couples the right to share their partner's health insurance if they weren't married. So we can only share health benefits if we're married, but we shouldn't be allowed to get married. He's also said that gay people shouldn't be teachers, as I'm sure you're aware."

"Yeah," Jonathan said wearily. "He hasn't always been this way. In his defense, I will say that he's smart and ambitious. He knows what to say to win over a crowd."

"So he's not actually a conservative homophobe?"

"Well. I'm from fucking Kansas. I mean, I was really young when he got elected to the House, so I grew up mostly in DC, but my father was raised in a pretty rural town about thirty miles outside of Wichita. He represents old farmers and small-town folks. Some of them have outdated ideas. He's cultivated his public persona to appeal to that." He sighed. "I didn't want to say anything on the record, but I frequently disagree with him. We fought a lot when I was a teenager. He's not the sort of man you can win an argument against. But you'd have to ask him how much of what he says he actually believes."

It was hard for me to let go of my resentment of the Senator, but I tried to see him as Jonathan must have. Richard Granger was, after all, a man, a husband, a father, a real person, and not a supervillain.

Jonathan played with his fork and said, "I suspect my mother had undue influence on him too. You probably know that the Blethwyns made most of their money in the sixties and seventies, and Mom wants to hang on to it. I think that's a big reason why Dad's a Republican. My family has dabbled in Kansas politics for years and was never especially conservative until Dad took that crazy right turn, but even then he used to be more level-headed, more fiscally than socially conservative. He moves a little further right every year. But I don't know if he even believes half the stuff he says out loud. I'm pretty sure that these days, he believes what he thinks will get him elected."

That didn't really raise my estimation of him much. "I don't understand you," I said.

"What don't you understand?"

"Why do you live for this man? The fact that you're even sitting here with me right now shows that you're at least a little bit more open-minded than he is. So why does it matter what your father says or does? Why don't you carve out your own life? Plenty of politicians' kids live perfectly normal lives out of the spotlight."

"It's complicated. He's my father, I don't know. He says—"

"Fuck him."

Jonathan furrowed his brow in frustration. "I can't explain it any better than that," he said. He was saved from having to talk more when the waiter brought out our dinners.

We ate in silence for a while. I was good and irritated, so I opted to keep my mouth shut. Actually, if anything, the whole situation made me sad. We finally had everything out in the open, I thought, and where did it leave us? I still liked him, for reasons I didn't understand. He liked me. He was definitely gay, denials or not. Yet we were getting nowhere. Then I noticed he was staring at me.

"What?" I asked. "Why are you looking at me like that?"

"No reason." His face went neutral. "I'm sorry about my father."

"You are not your father. It's not up to you to apologize."

He took a bite of his fish. "Can I ask you a personal question?"

"Sure, why the hell not?"

He went back to staring at me, which I found unnerving, so I went back to eating. He said, "Do you really feel that being gay is a part of who you are as a person?"

The question caught me off guard. "Yeah," I said, lifting my voice at the end of the word to imply a question.

"But if you were straight, it wouldn't be."

"I disagree. I think your sexuality is always a part of who you are, gay, straight, whatever. Besides, I'm out. The column I write for the *Forum* is on gay culture, which I assume you've figured out by now. I get hired for writing gigs *because* I'm gay. It's a part of me whether I want it to be or not."

"Does that ever freak you out?"

"Maybe a little, but on the other hand, I don't have to hide who I am." I narrowed my eyes at him.

"I'm not gay."

"So you keep saying."

"There's nothing… obviously gay about you."

"What the hell is that supposed to mean?"

"I mean, I guess the way you talk, kind of, but—"

And that was kind of the last straw. I got mad and slammed my fork on the table. "What? Am I supposed to be limp-wristed and have a lisp and call everyone 'girlfriend'? I *am* gay in all the ways that matter. There's really only one thing you have to have in order to be a member of the family, and that's the desire to fuck other men. That's a test I pass for sure." It was maybe a little harsh, but man, it felt good to say aloud.

Jonathan shook his head, suitably chastened. "I'm sorry. I'm an idiot."

I smiled ruefully. I managed to talk myself down; I knew he was asking me in an effort to make his own life make sense. I said, "No, it's all right. Look, you are who you are. I am who I am. I'm a writer, a friend, a son, a gay man. But if it makes you feel better, my ex and I marched in the Pride parade last year, I like fashion, I like showtunes, I have a good friend who's a drag queen, and I own several pink shirts. I look very good in pink."

"I'll bet you do," said Jonathan.

We wrapped up dinner and sojourned over to Teddy's, a gay bar on Avenue B that showed *Brooklyn Heights* every week, mostly because the owner, the eponymous Teddy, had a big crush on Rey. I'd brought Rey to the bar once to introduce them, and Teddy had gone apoplectic. This worked out for me, because I got drinks on the house whenever Teddy was there. Which he was when I dragged in Jonathan.

I needed the beer Teddy offered. As we sat at the bar, I was feeling raw, hurt, and pretty annoyed. I'd gotten to Jonathan, I'd seen it on his face, but his continued refusal to acknowledge what we both knew was the truth was incredibly frustrating. That I cared so much was maybe even more frustrating. But once the show started, we stopped speaking of it. We sipped beer and watched television as if we'd spent dinner talking about the weather.

The camera was eating Rey right up during most of this episode, lingering over him during a particularly heated conversation he had with his costar. Then they started making out, which culminated in Rey whipping his shirt off over his head before the scene faded to black. The whistles from other people in the bar indicated the audience appreciated that.

"Did Rey and that actress ever date?" Jonathan asked.

"Nah, she's married." I mentioned her husband, an actor who had peaked as a teen star in the 80s and had of late taken to starring on failed medical dramas on basic cable. "Rey did briefly date the actress who plays Rosie, but that didn't last very long."

Jonathan smirked at me. "Oh, and here I thought maybe you and Rey had…."

I laughed. The particulars of what I had and had not done with Rey were not something I wanted to discuss with Jonathan. "Rey is aggressively straight," I said instead of explaining.

This pulled a chuckle from Jonathan who, after a few drinks, had loosened up a bit.

Still, I was thinking that this was probably it. That Jonathan would go back to his life and his job and his land of denial and I would move on to greener, less-closeted pastures. That was easier said than done, though. Why did Jonathan have to be so attractive? His sand-colored hair was cut short and gelled within an inch of its life—that was something I wanted to dissuade him from doing—but he had an angular face with a wide mouth, and he had a marvelous body under that stupid polo shirt. That was bad enough, but I could compartmentalize attraction. I'd had enough crushes on straight guys that I could move past the physical. What really got to me was that even when we were arguing, something between us just clicked. And the dinner discussion hadn't even felt like an argument, more like a confession. Jonathan had been honest with me, at least, even if he couldn't be honest with himself. I knew I shouldn't touch this situation with a ten-foot pole, and yet I couldn't just end it, either. Not when I knew that Jonathan was just as attracted to me as I was to him.

When the episode ended, he said, "Wow. I can see why people like this show. Rey is great. I almost forgot he's Rey, you know? And I should hate his character. He's a liar and a cheat and you know he's going to break Wendy's heart. But he's so magnetic. You can't look away when he's on screen."

"I know," I said quietly.

Jonathan turned and gave me a questioning look.

I shrugged and stood up. "I should probably get going home."

"Yeah, me too."

"Where do you live?"

"I'm renting out the ground floor of a house in Boerum Hill."

"Oh. I've always liked Boerum Hill. How do you like it?" I walked outside, wincing at the wall of humidity that hit me as we left the air-conditioned bar. The weather clearly hadn't gotten the memo about it being fall.

"It's nice. I'm on Dean Street. It's a pretty neighborhood."

And then this bit of stupidity slipped from my lips: "Ah. Well, I'm not too far from there. Do you want to share a cab?"

"Sure, all right."

I was afraid to say anything important. I proposed walking towards First Avenue because it would be easier to get a cab there. I shoved my hands in my pockets to curb the temptation to touch him, and we walked in companionable silence, speaking only to comment on the temperature or to warn each other away from detritus on the sidewalk. When we got to First Avenue, I held up my hand and we got a cab fairly quickly. I directed the cabbie to go over the Brooklyn Bridge.

We hit traffic near Canal Street. Jonathan looked out the window and groaned. "Look at all the kids out. Clubbing on a Wednesday? Really?"

"Kids? Aren't you only twenty-five?"

"Twenty-six. Too old for that scene."

"Aw, come on. You didn't go through that phase when you were right out of college and finally living on your own, when you just went nuts? I remember being twenty-three and… God, I did a lot of stupid things."

"Yeah?" He looked like he wanted to ask what those stupid things were. I wasn't anxious to volunteer. A lot of going home with the wrong men, more risky sex than I was really willing to confess to. But Jonathan just said, "No, I never went through a phase like that."

"And yet you drink like a fish."

Jonathan sighed. "I was nervous tonight."

The parade of stupid continued when I heard myself ask, "Do I make you nervous?" Jonathan's eyes widened, which was all the answer I needed. Breaking through the Great Wall of Denial would be the challenge here. Whispering, I said, "My editor wanted me to out you in the article, but I couldn't do it. I want you to know that."

Jonathan closed his eyes. Then the light changed and the cabbie raced through the intersection at Canal Street and hit a pothole hard, jostling us passengers, who hadn't bothered with seat belts. I was pushed towards Jonathan, and I put out my hand to prevent myself from falling over his lap. Instead, my hand landed on his thigh, and when the cab was moving smoothly again, I found I was leaning against him, his face just inches from mine, our lips perfectly aligned.

"Uh…," Jonathan said.

I listened as the cabbie chatted in Arabic to the hands-free device in his ear. "That guy hardly speaks English. He doesn't know who you are."

"Doesn't change anything."

"It does. You can be someone else, if only for as long as you're in this cab."

"Who would I be?"

"Whoever you want, babe."

Jonathan parted his lips but didn't move closer. I was close enough that when I opened my mouth to say something else, my lips brushed against his. "Are you attracted to me?" I whispered.

"Drew, please don't—"

"It's a simple question."

"I...."

We hung there, mouths poised to touch, not moving, breathing hard. Then the cab pulled onto the bridge and jostled us together again. I smashed my lips against Jonathan's.

I was rewarded with a hungry response and a sound strangled somewhere in the back of his throat. This was right up there on my All-Time List of Stupid Things Done in the Heat of the Moment—a list that is legendary in its length—but I didn't care because Jonathan smelled like aftershave and good scotch and he was kissing me back fervently. It was the kind of kiss that made my blood rush. I was hard, some animal instinct kicked in, and I wanted to push him against the door and rip all his clothes off.

Except the cabbie cleared his throat and broke the moment, saying, "Where you want to go?"

I looked up and saw that we'd made it over the bridge.

"Dean and Bond," Jonathan said, pulling away.

I supposed I shouldn't have expected the invite in when we got to his place, but I was still disappointed when Jonathan tossed me a twenty and got out of the cab. I watched him go up to the house and then sighed and said, "Myrtle and Vanderbilt." The cabbie took me home.

CHAPTER
Eight

I HAD a spot in Prospect Park, at a picnic table near the band shell, where I ate lunch almost every day that the weather was nice. I worked out of my apartment, which I often found isolating and claustrophobic, so it was good to get outside.

Rey knew about this, so I was not surprised when he found me there a few days after The Kiss. He had on what I thought of as his Clark Kent disguise: Yankees cap over a pair of sunglasses. He still looked like himself, in my opinion, but he claimed he never got recognized this way. I thought the get-up made him more conspicuous.

On this particular day, I was eating a take-out salad out of a plastic container and reading a book I didn't like very much. Rey sat across from me and, with no introduction, said, "What are you reading?"

I didn't bother to look up. "The *Times* is finally letting me review another book. Unfortunately, I have no idea what I'm going to write in said review, because all I can think of to say about this one is 'it sucks, don't read it'."

"What's it about?"

I looked up and grinned. "Two close friends who live in New York."

"Ha," said Rey.

I went back to eating my salad. "Every last one of the characters in this novel is completely despicable. Naturally, one of them is gay, and that's the only reason I can think of why they sent it to me. Like now I'm some expert on gay literature. I guess that's what I get after I wrote that essay on Armistead Maupin a few months ago. But you didn't come here to ask about my latest assignment."

Rey shrugged. "I wound up bringing Britney to the *Brooklyn Heights* premiere. You remember Britney?"

So he was going to have to work up to whatever he had to say. Okay. "Vaguely. Was she the blonde you dated last year?"

"Yeah. I think she only agreed to go with me for the red carpet thing. We had dinner later and all she could talk about was meeting all the actors from the show."

"You live a strange life, my friend."

"Thanks for your help with the suit, by the way. Everyone said I looked great."

"Sure, what else are gay best friends good for than picking out clothes that make you look your best?" I grinned. Rey had a stylist on retainer, but he'd been unavailable, giving me the opportunity to fill in. "So is this where I'm supposed to do the guy thing and ask if you got laid?"

He laughed. "I got laid."

I cracked my knuckles. "See that? The suit is magic. Good to see I've still got the touch."

"Of course, she bailed the next morning and hasn't returned my calls, so, you know." He sighed. "Oh, but Allie called me."

I shook my head. "She is a foolish girl. What did she say?"

"Dunno." Rey reached over and picked a piece of chicken out of my salad. I hit him on the back of the hand with my plastic fork. "Ow!" He shook his hand. "Well, so… you're gonna get mad."

Oh, boy. "Try me."

"She made me swear not to say anything, but we, uh, spent a night together a few months ago, right before I left for Prague. So she called me the other night, I think as a booty call?"

"Oh, I wish I didn't know that." I put the salad aside, having lost my appetite. "I am never giving you the phone number of any woman ever again." Rey and Allie had been peripherally aware of each other for a long time, since I had met Allie in college, but to my knowledge, they hadn't ever been friends with each other. I didn't know what to do with the fact that my knowledge was wrong. I frowned at Rey.

"What? I didn't destroy her life or anything. We went out on one date months ago, I invited her over to my place, you don't need to know the details, and then we went our separate ways again. I've hardly talked to her at all since. I like her and all, but I don't think there's much of a spark between us, and she feels the same way. I think she just wanted to, I don't know, get it out of her system."

"Ugh." That sounded like Allie. She is one of those people who will try anything once, and I suspected she was happy enough to check "sex with a movie star" off her bucket list. "Well, for the record, I never thought this would happen."

"That what would happen? Me sleeping with Allie?"

I leveled my gaze at Rey. "You do realize that—and, seriously, it's like a sign of the apocalypse—this means we have a person in common that we've both slept with."

Rey turned a little green. "Oh, God. I forgot about that."

"It wasn't one of my prouder moments. I bet it was a much different experience with you."

And let that be a lesson. The short version is that I was really drunk one night in college. Allie came on to me. I thought it might be an interesting experiment to see if I was maybe not as gay as I thought. Turns out, I am really, really gay. Somehow, our friendship endured despite this ill-thought-out interlude.

"I hope it was better with me," Rey said. "Though I always thought she had kind of a thing for you."

"Yeah, in another lifetime. That night we… you know… that was a million years ago. She knows better now." I sighed. "You aren't going to sleep with her again, are you?"

"I told her I was busy when she called the other night. And now that you've reminded me of the Night That Shall Not Be Discussed, I am definitely not going to sleep with her again."

"Okay. Good."

Rey clucked his tongue. "You know, I'm not a bad boyfriend. I'm a nice guy. I always treat women well. I mean, what if I really liked Allie? Hypothetically. Would you still tell me not to see her?"

I didn't know the answer for that. The truth was that I probably would. "I don't know," I said. "It doesn't matter if you aren't going to sleep with her again. Can we talk about something else?"

"What, like you have a love life to discuss?"

"Maybe I do," I said defensively.

Rey's eyebrows shot up in surprise. "Explain."

This was not going to be a fun conversation. I picked at some of the old paint on the picnic bench. "The good news is that I'm not obsessing over Aaron anymore."

"That *is* good," Rey said. He was, generally, uncomfortable discussing my sex life, but he was a good sport about it. "Did you meet someone new?"

"Kind of," I said.

"Who is he? Do I know him?" When I nodded, he asked, "Is it that soccer player we ran into at Pastis a few weeks ago?"

Wow, I had forgotten all about that guy. I had ruled him out because he looked too much like Aaron. But good to know Rey was paying attention. I took a deep breath. Might as well get it out there, I thought. "No. This week, my heart belongs to one Jonathan Granger."

Rey nearly toppled off the bench. "What? Jonathan? Jonny? My cousin Jonny? Son of the scary, wants-to-eradicate-you-and-your-kind senator? Guy-I-told-you-to-stay-away-from Jonathan? How the hell did that happen?"

I couldn't tell if he was angry or not. He looked more shocked than anything. I said, "In my defense, he gave me his number. And you know me, that's like a dare. We went out Wednesday, on the pretense of celebrating the article I wrote. I guess I haven't had the chance to tell you. It kind of turned into a date... or, I don't know. I assume Jonathan hasn't mentioned it."

Rey winced. "No. I talked to him yesterday, actually, and he didn't mention that he'd seen you at all. Despite what you said, I really didn't know he was gay. In fact, I was pretty sure of the opposite."

"Surprise!" I sat forward and rubbed my face. "I told myself I wouldn't date any more closeted guys. It's just too much work."

"But... are you sure? He told me he's been kind of seeing a teacher at his school. A female teacher."

That surprised me. He hadn't mentioned seeing anyone. "Oh, I'm sure he's gay. And he hates himself for it too. He's one of those guys who will swear he's straight while he's got your dick in his mouth."

"Drew."

"Just saying."

"Did you two, ah...." Rey gestured vaguely.

"No. I kissed him, and he kissed me back, for the record, and it was very good, and then he panicked."

"You kissed." Rey looked nauseous again.

I ignored his unease. "I should be able to just walk away, you know? I should say, 'No, he's too much trouble', and get on with my life. A relationship with him is doomed to fail, because he'll never be able to reconcile who he is with who he thinks he's supposed to be. Even if he were willing to acknowledge that he's gay, he'll never come out publicly because of who his father is. I don't need that. I don't want to have a secret affair and I don't want to get pulled back into the closet. I just want a normal relationship, dammit, or as normal a relationship as I'm capable of having, where I don't have to hide or conduct business in secret locations, you know?" Angry with myself, I slammed my book shut. "Anyway, I haven't heard from him at all since Wednesday, so I guess it's over."

"But?"

"I like him a lot, Rey. More than anyone who's come along in a while."

"What are you going to do?"

"Nothing. I'm not going to call him."

"What if he comes to you?"

"That's kind of what I'm afraid will happen. But I don't think he will."

Rey looked off at something in the distance. We sat together quietly for a while. We'd been friends for more than half our lives, and yet there were still these things we had trouble talking about.

I said, "Are you mad? That I went out with Jonathan, I mean."

He sighed. "No, I guess not. It just seems like a bad idea." He looked at me. "Not just because he's my cousin. I mean, you don't want me to go out with your friends because that kind of changes the dynamic of your friendship, right? Same with you and Jonathan."

A valid point. "Yeah."

"I also, you know, don't want you to get hurt. Just. I mean. You know."

I had to smile. Rey was not very good with the emotional stuff.

"But," he said, "I don't know, maybe you'd be good together."

I looked at Rey. He looked pensive. Was he giving me permission to date his cousin? That seemed weird. "Are you...?"

"This is a lot to process. I haven't really decided how I feel about it, but I can't tell you what to do. I mean, it's not my place, first of all, but you'd just do what you wanted anyway." He rubbed his face.

"I guess I can't stop you from dating my friends, either." I ran a hand through my hair. This was as close as we were going to get to having a moment.

True to form, Rey changed the subject. "So I got an interesting script in the mail last week."

"Yeah?"

"Yeah. Sort of a dark comedy about a man who keeps dating the wrong women."

I grimaced. "Gee."

"The script is really well written. And the director attached to the project wants to film in New York, so that would be convenient. It's a really good role. I think I could do well at it."

"That's good, then."

"If all goes to plan, shooting would start before we finish filming *Brooklyn Heights*, but I think I can still do it because I'm not in the last few episodes much. So I have to decide if I want to take this part."

"What's to decide? Take it. It sounds like a good opportunity."

More silence followed. Rey watched some kids tossing a basketball back and forth on the blacktop near the band shell. I picked at the picnic table with my fork.

Sensing our conversation was drawing to a close and needing to get back to my work, I started gathering up my things. "Not to bail on you, but I need to get going. You need anything, you call me, all right?"

"Yeah. Same goes." After a long pause, he said, "You knew he was gay the whole time, didn't you?"

I nodded. I felt him watching me.

As I was about to leave, he said, "You must really like him if you knew but still didn't out him in your article."

"Yeah." That was the truth, wasn't it? "Partly I didn't do it for the sake of your family."

"I don't believe you. And anyway, don't worry about my family. Uncle Richard could certainly use the wake-up call."

CHAPTER
Nine

I WAS pulled out of deep sleep by someone pounding on my door. Thinking it was an emergency, I bolted out of bed and ran to answer it. I do not think I would have been more surprised if the President of the United States had been standing on the landing outside my door.

Instead of the leader of the free world, it was Jonathan. And there I was, wearing only ratty pajama pants.

He had on a pair of tight jeans and a green T-shirt that clung to his chest. He looked edible. In my sleepy haze, I thought maybe I'd imagined him. Then he spoke.

"You were sleeping. I'm so sorry." He didn't look especially sorry, though, and he certainly didn't move to leave.

I didn't quite have the mental capacity to form solid thoughts, but I managed to say, "It's all right. What is it?"

"Can I come in?"

"Uh, okay." My confusion was a tangible thing, a cloud blocking the synapses in my brain from firing correctly. I turned and walked into my apartment. I heard Jonathan follow and close the door behind him. I turned around when I was in the middle of the living room. "I sure as hell didn't expect to see you again. Now, what—?"

He didn't give me a chance to finish the question. He kissed me instead.

He tasted like whiskey. That was the first thing I noticed. Then it clicked that this was Jonathan, who swore he wasn't gay, kissing me in my apartment with everything he had. I put a hand on his chest and found his T-shirt to be a little clammy, but the warmth of his skin beneath it held some promise.

Except that this was going to end badly. I pulled away and took a step back. "Oh, Jesus." I was definitely awake now. I turned again and walked into my kitchen. Jonathan followed, his sneakers squeaking on the linoleum.

I said, "You know, it would be better for everyone if you just picked up some guy in a bar and got your needs met. Use a fake name, put in colored contacts, fuck the first pretty boy who comes your way."

"I don't want some guy," Jonathan said with a conviction that surprised me. "I want you."

I tried to remind myself that despite my sense that something inevitable was going on, I still had the power to put a stop to it. I pulled my water pitcher out of the fridge and then took two glasses out of the cabinet. I poured water for each of us. "How drunk did you have to get to come to that conclusion?"

He stood there, his face wrinkled up in a parody of deep thought, like he was working out a complicated mathematical equation. I handed him a glass of water, which he took. By the time I put the pitcher back in the refrigerator, he still hadn't spoken.

"Fine, don't answer that," I said. "I'll try something easier. How did you get my address? I don't recall giving it to you."

"I called Rey."

"Ah. Remind me to kill him later."

"I've pissed you off now."

While I *was* angry that he'd had to get drunk before coming to see me, a part of me was really happy to see him again. "No, I'm not pissed at you. I'm angrier at myself."

"Why?"

I downed all of the water in my glass and then put the glass in the sink. Glass and metal collided with a clang. "For even contemplating going to bed with you."

"Oh," said Jonathan. He downed his water too.

"That is why you came over here, right? Or did you feel it necessary to tell me again how not gay you are?"

"No, I—"

I didn't wait for his response. "Everything in me is screaming that you're bad news. That I should have nothing to do with you. That whole closeted-guy thing—been there, done that, bought a postcard. It's not fair to either of us to get involved in that. And I will not be anyone's drunk mistake."

"I'm not that drunk," he said. He handed his glass back to me, and I put it in the sink.

"I don't want to be the man you have to get drunk to sleep with, either."

"I'm not—"

"But you had a few before coming over here."

He shrugged.

"God, Jonathan. Just being friends with you takes all the self-control I have. I know I shouldn't get involved with you, and yet I can't bring myself to push you away. And now you're giving me this look like you want to eat me for dessert—which I guess you just admitted you do—and it's all I can do not to jump you right here in this kitchen."

Jonathan stood there with his head cocked for a moment. I could almost see the gears turning in his alcohol-addled brain. Then he reached for me and I let him. He put a hand on either side of my face then pulled me down for a kiss. I groaned with lust and regret and I kissed him and ran my fingers through his hair. His hands moved down my arms and slid around my waist.

"We're both going to regret this in the morning," I said.

"I won't." He didn't sound convinced.

I was a goner. I was too intrigued, too confused, and too aroused to resist him.

The most surprising thing was that he knew what to do. I'd been expecting, should this moment ever present itself, to have to coach him through it, but he knew his way around my body the way no straight guy had any business knowing. His hands roamed all over me, knew exactly where to touch me to bring me pleasure. There was nothing tentative about his touch, and every move was soothing and deliberate. Maybe the alcohol gave him confidence he wouldn't have had otherwise, but to me, what his movements said were that he'd had sex with a man before, clearly. I supposed that should have surprised me less than it did. I thought briefly of Wade's source—a spurned former lover, perhaps—but then pushed it out of my mind.

He peeled off his clothes on the way to my bedroom. I thought maybe he was in such a hurry because he worried he'd lose his nerve or change his mind, but as we toppled onto the bed, I in my pajama pants and he in only his underwear, it seemed clear that his mind was made up. I found that incredibly exciting, that he wanted me so badly he could push through his inhibitions. I wanted him with the same fervor.

The man could kiss too. He never held anything back. His kisses were wet and eager, and I loved how he tasted, like whiskey and man. His lips were perfect, smooth and thin and elegant just like the rest of him. Every time he nipped at my skin it felt like a tiny electric shock.

I decided to let him take the lead, and I let him push me onto my back as he planted kisses from my collarbone to my navel, leaving behind a trail of goose bumps. I couldn't hold back the groan as his body grazed my now-hard cock on the way down.

It was Jonathan who made the first big move, yanking my pajama pants down my legs in one fluid movement. There was no hesitation at all. I watched in awe as he closed his mouth around my cock. He bobbed his head up and down a few times, and his mouth was heavenly, warm and slick, and every movement sent little sparks through my body. I closed my eyes and surrendered to it until

I felt his curious and invasive fingers get into some inappropriate places. I wondered exactly what he thought he was up to. I was happy enough to lay there under his ministrations, though I was hard and aching and needing just a little bit more. I bucked against him, but he kept sucking at me gently. Hoping to spur him on, I reached for the drawer in my nightstand.

"If you're going to do that, you might need some help," I said, out of breath enough that the words came out stilted. I pulled a bottle of lube out of the drawer and tossed it to him. He caught it in one hand and looked at the bottle for a long moment before upending it and squirting some of the liquid on his other hand. Then he wrapped those long, graceful fingers around my cock and started to stroke. I gave up all pretense of expectation at that point; I had no idea what he would do next. I found I liked that this was the case.

He gave me a few long strokes, the lube warming as his hand moved over my dick. *That* was it, I thought, now we were getting somewhere. He moved to lie next to me, and we kissed again as he continued to stroke me. I think my brain started liquefying. I wanted to explain that there were other places the lube needed to go if this were going to be a successful coupling. My mouth would only make incoherent garbles, though, because what he was doing felt so divine. On other hand, if I didn't intervene, I was going to come, and then it would be all over before it really got started.

I just assumed that he'd want to fuck me. The thing was, I'd always preferred pitching to catching. I found, however, that with Jonathan, I would have done anything he asked. I wanted him that badly. But the real shocker in a long night of surprises came next.

He said, "I want you inside me."

I groaned. There were no words for how much I wanted that too. I pushed at Jonathan and got him onto his back, mostly out of self-defense. I was so charged up, I needed a moment to regain my composure. I grabbed his wrists and pushed them into the mattress, each on either side of his head. He left his arms there when I let go, and he watched me as I rubbed my hands along his whole torso, loving the feel of the wispy blond hairs on his chest against my palms. I pinched both of his nipples, and he cried out and arched off the bed. Then I grabbed his boxers and yanked them off, and his cock, hard and heavy, bobbed as I did so. I tossed his undies over my head. I grabbed the lube and poured some over my hands. Then I touched him.

No doubt about it, Jonathan was beautiful, in the Greek-god-statue sense, an excellent model of a male: muscular torso, a smattering of chest hair, hard cock red and throbbing. I placed my hand around his cock and stroked. His body arched again, and he made this keening, humming sound. He let out a breath and looked at me. I looked into his amazing greenish eyes. They shone in the dim lighting of my bedroom. He was naked, and not just in the physical sense.

I figured that I should go slow. I moved my hand and cupped his balls, which earned me a hiss; then I moved to the space behind them, gently probing without pushing inside, taking my time to learn his body and his reactions. He made these incredible little noises, grunts and sighs mostly. Soon he was begging me for more, begging for me to put my fingers inside him. I reached for the drawer again and pulled out a condom, covering myself before I lost control over the situation—which I seemed to be at constant risk of doing—then I slid a lubed-up finger inside him.

Watching his reactions stirred up something in me, aroused me more than I would have expected. His eyes were shut tightly, and he groaned as I slid in and out of his body. Then he got louder as I added a second finger. He writhed on the bed. I curled my fingers a little and found his prostate. A guttural moan escaped his lips as his hips jumped off the bed. I scissored my fingers to stretch him, and he grunted and twisted his fists in the sheets. I don't know when I've ever seen anything as beautiful, and knowing that I was the one making him writhe like that made my pulse race and my cock yearn for more.

"I need you near me," he murmured.

I pulled out my fingers, then pushed his legs up and apart. He put a hand behind each of his knees and held himself open for me. I moved between his legs and held my cock at his entrance. "Are you sure?" I asked.

"Yes," he panted. "Please. Now."

I pushed inside slowly, struggling not to pump my hips when instinct told me to do so. I felt Jonathan's body resisting me. He was tight, and the way he squeezed me made my whole body feel like it was roaring. I held back, unwilling to hurt him, but Jonathan kept pleading, so I moved achingly forward. Soon I was all the way inside him, and everything was tight and slippery and warm and wonderful. I bent my body to kiss him. He put his arms around me and groaned into my mouth. His whole body vibrated around me, and I saw sparks every time his muscles squeezed me. He got his hips into the action, pushing against me, begging me to move faster.

So I did. He hissed and dug his nails into my back. I found a rhythm that seemed to bring both of us the most pleasure, but I had to hold back a little, wanting to come after he did. I didn't have to wait long, luckily, because he started grasping at me, pulling my hair, moaning my name. He kissed me deeply, our tongues tangling. Then I felt him stop breathing. He came between us, hot and sticky on our stomachs.

I lost it. I pulled him into my arms and I rubbed my face in his hair, and I was completely overwhelmed by the sensations of his body pulsing around me, of the way he smelled and tasted. I pumped my hips one last time, then felt crazy, blind, and the orgasm hit me like a flash of lightning. I cried out as I came, surprised by the force of it, by how long it lasted. Then I collapsed on top of him.

We lay together for a long time afterwards, not speaking, just languishing in the moment. We were both sticky, sweaty messes, but it took a long time to regain the ability to use my limbs. I heard him breathing evenly, but his eyes were open, so he couldn't have been asleep. I didn't want him to freak out about what we'd just done. I willed him to be okay.

I don't know if I was getting uneasy vibes off him or if it was my own feeling self-conscious, but either way, I was itchy, so I got out of bed and went to the bathroom. I took care of the condom and cleaned myself off. I wet a cloth and went back to Jonathan. I cleaned him off while he watched me, and I wanted to know what he was thinking, but I was too afraid to ask. Completely unsettled, I stumbled back to the bathroom, tossed the cloth in the sink, and then walked back to the bed. He moved over to make space for me, so I lay beside him on my back and stared at the ceiling.

"Can I ask you something?" he said after a prolonged silence.

"Okay."

"You've always known you were gay."

Of all things. "Pretty much," I said. Which was close enough to the truth. I'd known from a fairly early age that there was something different about me, that I wasn't quite like the other kids. I thought I was broken somehow when my male friends started becoming interested in girls but I didn't. Then, not long after Rey and I met, we went to see a movie together, and I found that the male lead—I can't even remember who he was, some nobody who was cast more for his looks than his acting chops—made me think of unspeakable things. My thought process basically went like this: "*Oh... fuck.*"

Jonathan said, "Did you ever try sex with women?"

I sighed. "My friend Allie and I... one time in college."

"And?"

"And nothing. It was awkward and weird." I tried to come up with the best way to explain it. Although, of course, he must have understood also. "I feel the same way about sex with women as I do about yoga. I can see why some people would find it appealing, but it's just not for me."

He giggled. "Ah, okay. So that time with Allie, was that when you lost your virginity?"

Oh, Jonathan. I found him charmingly naive. I laughed. "That was my first and only time with heterosexual vaginal intercourse, yes. But I had sex for the first time when I was seventeen with my very first boyfriend, Pete."

"What was that like? The first time?"

I didn't know what to make of the twenty questions. I turned to look at him. The expression on his face was earnest, like he didn't have an agenda, he was genuinely curious. "The first time with Pete? Clumsy. Neither of us really knew what we were doing. They don't really teach you that in health class, you know? We spent the whole summer between high school and college just experimenting, seeing what felt good."

Jonathan moved a little closer to me, so I reached for him and pulled him into my arms. He rested his forehead against my cheek.

"We, uh, figured it out by the end of the summer," I said.

He reached out a hand and laid it on my chest. I liked how his slightly hairy arms looked against my skin, which was basically bare. (I'd somehow gotten to thirty still looking like an underdeveloped teenager as far as body hair went, so I'd taken to getting everything waxed. Being deliberately hairless seemed less embarrassing.)

"What happened to Pete?" Jonathan asked.

"Eh, nothing. He went to college in California. We loved each other in our fumbling teenage way, but we also both knew we'd never be able to maintain a relationship across the country. I still get the occasional card or e-mail from him, though. He settled in San Francisco and got married while it was legal to do so in California. He and his boyfriend—now husband, I guess—have been together for six years or something like that."

"Wow."

"Yeah, I can't even fathom that. I have a real knack for picking exactly the wrong guy to fall for, and so I have thus far not been that successful with long-term relationships. The longest was with Aaron, and that was only a year and a half or so."

"Aaron?"

Yeah, that was a sob story that would have to wait. "You don't need my whole relationship history right now."

"But you've been with a lot of men."

"A few."

"How did you know I was gay?"

I laughed. I couldn't help it. "Oh, honey. You gave me the Gay Gaze the first time I met you."

"What?"

I shifted on the bed a little to turn sideways and face Jonathan. "When you meet a straight guy, he kind of gives you the once-over. Then you shake hands and move on. If he's an alpha-male type, he'll look you in the eyes when he shakes your hand, but otherwise, it's all very efficient. He looks at you to get the information he needs to judge you, then he looks away. When you meet a gay man, the gaze lingers. It's a completely different kind of observation. It's less 'what do I need to know about this person' and more 'do I find this man attractive?' My favorite corollary is what I call the Shopping Double-Take. You'll be walking through a store and then you'll look up to find yourself looking at the face of a man. The two of you will pass each other. If the guy's straight, he'll keep walking, but if he's gay, he'll glance back over his shoulder for a better look."

"I never noticed before."

"Because you never wanted to be a part of that dating pool. Although you probably do it anyway without being conscious of it. You were definitely checking me out that night we had dinner at Rey's."

"Not deliberately."

"Even so. I could tell you were attracted to me."

"Don't be smug," Jonathan said, laughing.

I pulled him closer and kissed his forehead. "Or else it was wishful thinking on my part. I was checking you out plenty too. And I don't often fall for straight guys."

"I'm here, aren't I? That would show some very not-straight tendencies."

"True."

He pushed up so that he was looking down at me. "You were attracted to me? Right from the beginning?"

"Oh, yeah."

"That's crazy," he said.

"Why?"

"Because you're this smart, funny, interesting man in the body of an underwear model, and you're attracted to me? I'm… short and plain and—"

I put my fingers on Jonathan's lips. "There's nothing plain about you." I traced lazy trails over the planes of his face with my fingers. "You need to lay off the hair gel, but you've got a great face. And a great body."

Jonathan blushed and looked away.

"You know what else I noticed?" I put a hand on his face and gently nudged it back to face me. "You've done this before."

"Done what?"

"Now don't you get coy. You've slept with a man before. Here I thought I'd have to give a PowerPoint presentation with illustrations and diagrams, but you just dove right in feet first. For which, trust me, I am quite thankful, but there's no way you just knew what to do by instinct."

"I haven't been with another man since college."

And there it was, the big dirty secret. "Let me guess. You thought at the time that you were experimenting."

He shifted on the bed so that he was lying on his side, facing me. "Something like that. I mean, it started with a friend who called himself 'bi-curious'. We got roaring drunk one night and wound up naked, and then we…." He made a lewd gesture, which was shocking and kind of funny coming from him. He went on, "I liked it, so we did it again. I never thought of myself as gay. Believe me, I know how ridiculous this sounds, but this guy, he got plenty of pussy too. We talked about women a lot. Same deal with the next guy I slept with. I know this isn't logical, but that made it okay, knowing that the men I was seeing were into women too. I see now that there was a lot of denial going around. And then I graduated, and my dad had somehow gotten wind of some of what I'd been up to in college, and he gave me a lecture about public image and how I was to behave, and that was it, I stopped sleeping with men. Until tonight."

"And instead you got plenty of pussy."

"I guess. Not a lot, but I slept with a few women. Except I was starting to think I needed a Viagra prescription, because God. This woman from work. We went out one night a few weeks ago. I got really drunk, I let her talk me back to her apartment, and then I couldn't get it up. I blamed it on the alcohol at the time." He sighed. "I mean, I knew the real reason, but I didn't want…." He shook his head.

I felt for him, which was why I didn't push it too far. Part of me wondered how deep his denial really went.

I said, "That's why you didn't mention her in our interview, right? Rey told me you told him you were seeing a woman you worked with."

"Yeah. I was so embarrassed. I didn't want you to talk to her." He closed his eyes. "And I didn't want you to think I was interested in her because, well…."

He blushed. It was heart-melting. I kissed him. He kissed me back with a lot of enthusiasm, and then I felt him grow hard again against my leg.

"Well, clearly, you don't need the Viagra prescription," I said. Jonathan closed his eyes and sighed. I combed a hand through his hair. "Just go to sleep for now. We'll talk more in the morning. Okay?"

"Yeah," said Jonathan.

I WOKE up when the bed shifted. It took me a moment, but two things became clear: one, it was morning, and two, Jonathan was sitting hunched over at the edge of the bed, and his body language was not that of a happy man.

"Morning," I said.

He started and turned around. His jaw went slack.

"You know," I said, "when someone extends the courtesy of letting you stay in his dwelling overnight, it's best not to look completely horrified in the morning."

He closed his mouth and frowned. "I'm sorry."

I groaned. I so did not have patience for this. "Feels a little different when you're sober, huh?" Regret reared its ugly head. And it wasn't even that I regretted the sex, per se, it was more that Jonathan would regret it and now it would be a Big Deal and this was a situation I should have stayed away from.

I rolled over, tossed off the sheet, and then climbed out of bed. I was naked and half aroused, and I felt completely exposed in a way that I didn't like. Why did I do these things to myself? Why did I always make these bad decisions?

Jonathan sat on the bed staring at me. I knew at any minute he would bolt right out of my apartment. And that was almost more than I could bear. I went to my dresser and pulled out a pair of underwear and put them on.

"Look," I said, trying to get a handle on this situation. On top of the lingering shame and regret, now I was mad at Jonathan for pulling me into this mess to begin with. He was the one who'd come to me, right? He'd started it. "Everything is brighter in the morning. I'm aware of that. But this is fucking ridiculous. I know you weren't drunk that last time we had sex. It's pretty fucking insulting for you to still be pretending to be put off by me." I turned and fished a T-shirt out of a drawer. I had to cover myself up. I slid the shirt on and turned around again. "You, Jonathan, are a gay man. You always were a gay man. You will always be a gay man. You can deny it all you want. You can sleep with as many women as you want. That doesn't make it any less true."

Jonathan just sat there looking stunned, which was maybe the most unnerving thing. Then he seemed to snap out of it. He closed his eyes and swallowed. "Drew, please stop," he said. "I wasn't going to... I'm not... I mean, I'm sorry, but...."

"Fuck you, Jonathan." I stormed out of the room.

I went to the kitchen and started going through the motions of starting a pot of coffee. I was so distracted that I forgot to put water in the machine, so it beeped at me when I tried to make it start. By then, Jonathan had emerged from my bedroom. He stood at the kitchen door.

"Drew, I'm sorry," he said. "You've completely misinterpreted the situation, though."

"Have I?" I couldn't look at him. I didn't want to see his shame. "There doesn't seem to be much to misinterpret. You got drunk last night and thought it would be a good idea to come on over to ol' Drew's place, hoping to get laid, and I went right along with it because I'm a fucking idiot, and I know better than to get involved with closet cases like you, and I did it anyway because I wanted you so bad." And that was when I realized how much his rejection of me hurt. It hurt a whole goddamn lot. Because we'd talked and laughed and had mind-blowing sex most of the night. But he was about to bail. "And now you're going to apologize," I said, really martyring it up now. "You're going to tell me it was all one big mistake and we should forget about it and move on with our lives. Which, you know, I could do. I could totally chalk it up to a one-night stand and have that be the end of it." I slammed the coffee carafe on the counter before I turned around. Surprisingly, it didn't break. "Except, goddamn it, I don't want your apologies. I like you. I have no idea why, but I do. And it's going to suck a lot when you leave."

"Drew. Please, don't." I finally looked at him. His eyes were wide. "Okay. Okay. Yeah. I do want to apologize, but not for what you think. I'm sorry I upset you this morning. You caught me in a bad moment. Listen to me, though. I regret a lot of the things I've done in my life. I wish that things had been different to this point. Hell, I wish a lot of things. You can probably guess what some of those are. I'm sorry that this is so hard for me. I'm sorry that this is so hard on you. But I will tell you one thing I am not sorry for. I am not sorry I came here last night."

I think I probably stood in disbelief for a good minute before I could make words. So, fine, he wasn't regretting the sex, maybe, but he was still in the closet, and that was still a problem. I let his words hang in the air for a moment, and then I said, "Well, fuck."

"Yeah," he said. "I'm not like you, Drew. I didn't know what the hell was wrong with me for most of my life. Gay, that was never an option. So I hide. I don't talk about it. But it's like you... found me."

"So what the hell are we supposed to do now?"

"I don't know. I want to keep seeing you, but... I can't be seen with you."

I scoffed. "I've already told you. I don't like hypocrisy. And I'm not going back into the closet."

"I'm not asking you to, I just... I need some time. I really like you, too, and I want to see you again. If this is real, I'm the one who has to deal with everything." He looked up at the ceiling. "I need to be the one to tell my father. Before it hits the papers. You didn't out me, but that doesn't mean the next reporter I talk to won't. And I know better than to think no one will find out if I get involved in a relationship."

"All right," I said, trying to calm down. It didn't escape my notice that the easier solution for him was to just not get involved in a relationship. "That's something, I guess. You will tell your father?"

"Yes."

"Not even for my sake. You need to tell him for yours. Even if this thing with us never goes anywhere, you can't keep hiding. It will only get worse later."

"Yes. I know."

I let out a breath and looked down at my feet. I looked up again and noticed for the first time since he'd walked out of my bedroom that Jonathan was still naked. How could I have missed that? Because as amazing as he'd looked the night before in my poorly lit bedroom, he was a piece of art in the sunlight that came in through the kitchen windows. I shouldn't have gotten involved with him, I knew that. But I couldn't stay away. "I'm going to regret this," I said, unable to take my gaze off his body.

"I hope not," said Jonathan.

"You're, uh, not wearing any clothes."

"Oh? I hadn't noticed."

I had to smile. "Ah, you're flirting with me. Already we're making progress."

It was Jonathan who reached for me, who held his arms out until I took a step forward, who folded me close to his body and held me there for a long time. I could feel the heat of his naked body. He smelled like sex and some flowery shampoo and the warm, masculine scent that was all Jonathan. Being naked, he couldn't hide his arousal, either.

"I guess that whole not-being-seen thing becomes moot if we never go outside," I said. Some bitterness leaked out.

Jonathan tilted his head and kissed me, sliding his hands under my T-shirt and running them over my chest. Someone moaned, but I couldn't tell which of us it was. He took a step back and started to pull me towards the bedroom.

"Guess the coffee can wait," I said.

CHAPTER
Ten

"I LIKE how you smell," said Jonathan. He curled closer to me on the bed and ran a hand down my arm, then pressed his nose to my shoulder and inhaled.

"Um, thanks."

"I don't know if it's your soap or if it's just you, but I like it." He kissed my shoulder.

I murmured appreciatively in response, closing my eyes and putting an arm around him. I liked how he smelled, too, but I didn't think it was necessary to talk about it. I liked how he tasted and how his warm body felt pressed against me too.

"You know what else I like?" Jonathan asked.

I opened one eye. "You talk too much, J."

He moved even closer, until his lips were near my ear. "This doesn't feel weird."

"What doesn't?" I asked, already knowing the answer.

"Being in bed with a man. It feels almost normal and natural."

"It *is* normal and natural."

"Sure, maybe for you."

I waited for Jonathan to speak again, and when he didn't, I said quietly, "It's not always easy."

Jonathan backed away a little and propped himself up on an elbow to look at me. "What?" he asked.

"I'm lucky in that my mother has always completely supported me. I think she knew I was gay before I did. I spent a whole month working up to telling her, and then one day I just walked into the kitchen while she was cooking dinner. I had this whole speech prepared, but instead I blurted out, 'Mom, I'm gay' and got ready to make a run for it. Like, had a backpack full of stuff packed to go to Rey's house, expecting the worst. And she just said, 'Yes, dear, I know', and that was that. Day after, she joined PFLAG. When I started getting harassed at school, she wrote angry letters to the principal and then the local paper."

"She sounds amazing."

"She is." I took a deep breath. "But it wasn't easy. I mean, I was scared. There are few things more terrifying than being a gay teenager, I think. I got a good taste of it when I was in my last year of high school. Pete and I were an item, we started going out on dates in public. I knew some people would have a problem with it, but I guess I was naïve. I didn't know how bad it would get. I mean, Rey had my back, and as long as my being gay was more of a theoretical thing, people left me alone. But when I had a boyfriend, people started harassing me. My mom talked to the principal, who did nothing. Then Mom started writing letters. The principal told her she was being an unreasonable harpy."

"Wow."

"And, you know, it's not always easy to just be me, either. I'm lucky in that I have family and friends who accept me for who I am, that I live in a city with lots of other gay people, but, you know, for every woman like my mother, there's a man like your father. For all the good times I have, I also have a lot of fear. I'm afraid of violence, of disease. You keep telling me that I could never understand what you're going through, but I get it. I *know* how hard it is. I know how terrifying it is. And I've known many men like your father."

Jonathan looked at me with some mixture of confusion and determination, his brows drawn together. "It almost seems foolish," he said.

I felt the laughter bubble up in me, odd after so somber a speech. "What seems foolish?"

"All this turmoil over something so easy. Just... lying here with you is making me forget why I didn't want to." He rolled over and shoved his face into a pillow. When he peeked out again, he said, "I don't want to have to face the world, though. Do I have to leave here ever?"

I draped myself over Jonathan and put my arms around him. "Nope."

THERE was no crisis *per se*, but I met Rey at our regular Crisis Lunch location for brunch. When he got there, he sat across from me and narrowed his eyes. "You look smug."

"Nice of you to give Jonathan my address."

Rey raised his eyebrows. "I'm impressed he made it to your place. He was pretty drunk when he called."

I squinted at Rey. "So you knew he was drunk and still thought it would be a good idea to send him my way."

"Hey, I almost didn't. I thought that giving him your address was like pushing him into a hornet's nest."

"Gee, thanks."

Rey laughed. "But then I thought, what the hell? If he even made it, you're resourceful. I figured you'd make the most of it until Uncle Richard showed up to lynch you."

I sat back as a waitress came by to pour coffee. When she was gone, Rey examined the tiny pitcher full of creamer.

"Well," I said. "I'd be angrier at you if the sex hadn't been so good."

"Oh." Rey crumpled up his face. "If you're having sex with my cousin, I really, really don't want to know the details."

"If, hypothetically, we had a whole lot of sex this weekend and continued to have a whole lot of sex in the future, would it be a problem for you? Hypothetically."

"Only if you insist on talking about it at length. Why else would it be?"

"Well, as you just pointed out, he is your cousin. And also, you told me to stay away from him."

"Yeah, and look how well you listened."

I grinned. "I have a fierce independent streak. Seriously, though, you don't have a problem with it, do you? Bros before hos and all that." I raised a fist in salute.

Rey sighed. "No, I guess I don't have a problem with it. It just seems like a bad idea."

"Oh, getting involved with Jonathan is a colossally bad idea. Even if I got him to come around to the idea that being gay is okay—and I think he'll get there eventually—I still have to deal with the fact that he sprung from the loins of Richard Granger."

Rey raised an eyebrow. "Are you okay with that?"

"Jonathan is not his father."

"Well, obviously." He doctored his coffee.

They made the coffee at this restaurant especially strong, which I appreciated after a weekend without sleeping a lot. I took a careful sip and watched Rey.

After a while, he frowned and said, "You remember when I applied to NYU?"

I wondered if this was a trick question. "You mean, do I remember sitting in the mall food court with you while you agonized over your application, or are you referring to something more abstract?"

He looked at me and frowned. "Actually, I was referring to how I got Dad to pay the application fee on the pretense that I was applying to the business school when I was actually applying to be a theater major. I was pretty sure I'd get away with that particular lie until graduation. Unfortunately, my father is not stupid."

I did remember that. There'd been a particularly vicious fight that went on for a week. I'd been really worried through that whole saga because Rey and I going to college together was part of The Plan, and I was upset when it looked like it might not happen. "Right," I said.

"You probably don't remember this, but Uncle Richard and Aunt Sadie and Jonny all came out to visit around the time I got my acceptance letter. Richard kept going on about how proud he was of me for doing well in school and getting into a good college, and he made a point to read the letter aloud while the whole family was assembled in the living room after dinner one night. Dad and I had already been fighting about it for a couple of days, and he was still trying to get me to go to business school so he hadn't wanted to bring up college at all, but Richard insisted. And Dad responded as you would have expected and got all, 'Oh, I'm glad Reynolds got into a good school, but he's not going to NYU, he's going to Yale and blah blah'." Rey sighed. "I got kind of argumentative, told him I didn't want to go to Yale, and Richard actually came to my defense. He said, 'Eh, let the kid go where he wants. If he wants to be an actor, let him'. That shocked the hell out of me at the time, but not because of who Richard is. I honestly thought all the adults would team up against me. I think that he had a talk with my dad later that night that might have gone a long way towards my actually being allowed to study acting."

"Really?"

"Yeah. Richard is a lot more open-minded than you'd think. He went through that same struggle with Jonny a few years later. He wanted Jonny to study law, but Jonny wanted to study physics. Although Jonny succumbed to the pressure a little and actually started Georgetown as a government major but changed after his first semester."

I wasn't sure what all this proved. "Doesn't that just show that Jonathan is afraid of his father? Probably with good reason?"

Rey shook his head. "The Senator has said some terrible things in public. I won't defend him for that. But I will say that he's not just Senator Granger. He's also Uncle Richard. He's the uncle who defended my choice of college majors to my father, who stuck up for me when I wanted to study acting. He also completely supported Jonny when Jonny decided not to go into law or politics. And, you know, he was never a neglectful parent. He made sure Jonny was always taken care of, that he did his homework on time, that he had fun. He always remembered everyone's birthdays. One time, when I was maybe twelve, he took me and Jonny to Busch Gardens, and I think he had more fun on the roller coasters than we did. He's just a man, under everything else."

I'd never heard any of this before. I'd been writing about Richard Granger for years, and never once had Rey stopped me to tell me I was wrong about his uncle. I wondered why he was only telling me all this now. I worried suddenly that I'd been offending Rey for all the years I'd been writing my column, but he'd just been too polite to say anything. "What's your point?" I suddenly felt defensive.

Rey took it in stride. "Richard has a public image to maintain, that's for sure, and if Jonny's gay, well, that complicates things a whole hell of a lot. But I don't think Richard is entirely the problem here. I have no doubt that he loves his son. Things would get complicated if Jonny came out publicly, but if he's hiding in the closet, I don't think the blame for that can be laid entirely at Richard's feet."

The waitress appeared. I had forgotten what I was supposed to do in a restaurant until the waitress started flirting with Rey and talked him into getting the French toast. I ordered an omelet that I didn't intend to do much more than pick at. I felt the truth in what Rey was saying, which didn't bode well for my future with Jonathan.

"You're awfully philosophical all of a sudden," I said when the waitress left.

"I'm just trying to put things in perspective."

I looked into my coffee cup and noticed it was empty. "Well, thanks for taking the wind out of my sails."

"I'm sorry."

"How come you've never said any of this before?"

Rey shrugged. "You've never been this involved with a member of my family before."

"Who says I'm involved?"

Rey raised an eyebrow. "You were involved the moment you first met him. If you weren't, you would have walked away weeks ago."

CHAPTER
Eleven

I STARED at the screen of my laptop and reread the same sentence I'd already read three times. My column was not coming along so easily that week. At Wade's suggestion, I was writing about a lesbian couple in Massachusetts that was getting divorced, or I was trying to write about them, but my heart wasn't really in it.

Instead, my mind wandered. I thought about the weekend I'd spent with Jonathan and how much fun it had been to just lay around in bed with him. I thought about how good the sex had been, the way he smelled, what it felt like to be inside him. I thought about Richard Granger, about all the things he'd said, the policies he stood behind, my principles. I thought about what Rey had said about the Senator being just a man. All of these things swam around in my head and made it impossible to focus, especially since I was writing about a couple whose relationship was falling apart, but I was on the verge of something just beginning.

On the other hand, Jonathan would be coming over in a little while, which cheered me up.

The phone rang and I picked it up without looking at the caller ID. "Drew's House of Hackery."

The caller laughed. "Having a hard time with your column?"

"Rob!" It had been a while since I'd heard from Rob, a friend from my NYU days. "Hey, you never call anymore. How are you?"

"I'm good. You sound pretty upbeat. That's good."

"Yeah, I'm doing pretty well these days."

"Good. Hal and I were talking about what to do tonight, and it came up in conversation that we haven't seen your ass out since what happened with Aaron. He was sort of afraid you'd done yourself in."

"No such luck." I was surprised to realize that I hadn't thought about Aaron in a few days. "Actually, I just started seeing someone new."

"That's great!" Rob said. "Who is he? Anyone I know?"

"No, I don't think so. He's new in town." I trusted Rob but wasn't sure that Jonathan's secret was mine to tell, so I didn't volunteer a name.

Rob said, "You should bring him out tonight. Hal wants to go dancing, so we're thinking about checking out this new place called Push in the Meatpacking District. Or we might just go to Rooster's." Rob hummed for a moment. "Actually, maybe we should just go to Rooster's. New clubs are always full of those twenty-two-year-old hipsters who chain smoke instead of eat. And being a thirty-year-old married guy, I'd just feel old."

I laughed. "God, I haven't been out in forever. I guess I was avoiding Aaron."

"Yeah, I know." Rob was quiet for a moment. "I've seen him around some."

I did not find that surprising. There were a lot of gay men in New York, but they all seemed to go to the same places. "Yeah?"

"He did you a favor," was all Rob said.

There was something in me that wanted to go out, that wanted to see Aaron to show him that I was doing well without him. It seemed unlikely that Jonathan would consent to go out with me, though, especially not to a gay club. "My, ah… the guy I'm seeing, we have plans tonight."

"So adjust them. Come out with us."

I sighed. "He's not so much into the club scene. I want to come out tonight, but I don't know if he'd be willing to come too."

"So don't give him a choice. Just bring him out. What's the point of dating someone if you don't go out together?"

What was the point indeed? "Maybe."

"Hal and I miss you. If we don't see you tonight, maybe we can get together for dinner or something next week. If you ask sweetly, Hal may even cook."

I laughed. How had it gotten to the point where I was not just avoiding mine and Aaron's places but all of the people we knew in common too? I felt like a paranoid fool. Rob was *my* friend; there was no reason to let Aaron have him in the breakup. "I've missed you guys too," I said.

"Seriously, think about coming out tonight."

"I will." And I gave it what I thought was a lot of consideration. When I got off the phone with Rob, I started to think that it was actually a good idea. I wanted to dance and I wanted to show off Jonathan. I wanted to prove that I was really okay. And I *was* okay. That was the surprising thing. The prospect of running into Aaron didn't scare me as much as it would have a few weeks before.

But talking Jonathan into going out would be difficult. He'd told me that he wanted to see me but didn't want to be seen with me. But maybe Rob was right, I thought. Maybe I should simply not give Jonathan a choice.

I was still in what I thought of as my writing clothes—a T-shirt and a pair of destroyed jeans that I should have thrown out eons before; I liked how they fit, though, so I never could throw them out—when Jonathan showed up a little while later.

"Hey, J," I said as I let him into the apartment.

"Hi." His gaze traveled the whole length of my body until it settled on my feet. I was barefoot. He stared. At length, he said, "You have really nice feet."

I laughed. "Well, there's a compliment. Thanks. My friend Allie and I went for pedicures yesterday."

"Pedicures?" Jonathan asked.

"And here you thought I never did anything stereotypically gay." I wiggled my toes, which Jonathan was still looking at. "See, from where I sit, being gay is actually quite freeing. There are plenty of straight guys who are too afraid to be perceived as anything less than 100 percent man, and thus they will never know the great pleasure that is a mani/pedi at the hands of Kim Lee. She's my Korean manicurist. She can do amazing things. I don't know this first hand, but I've heard a rumor that she can give you an orgasm just by touching this one spot on your foot."

"Wow," said Jonathan. Then he laughed and looked up at me.

I loved his smile. His teeth were basically perfect except for the front two, one of which overlapped the other. It was subtle, and you couldn't tell unless you spent as much time looking at his mouth as I did. He was like a bundle of these little imperfections that somehow came together to make a flawless whole.

Then I remembered my mission. "Say," I said. "You're a waist size what? Thirty-four?"

"Yeah, so?"

"We're going out."

His eyes widened. "What? I thought you said we were going to hang out here and watch a movie."

"Nope. I changed my mind. I've been cooped up here working for two days, and I was thinking all afternoon that I really wanted to go dancing tonight, that I haven't been out in forever. Like, really out, with people and flashing lights and the whole nine. And now you're here, I have someone to go out with. But you can't go out in that."

Jonathan looked down at himself. He had on a blue polo shirt and khakis. "What's wrong with what I'm wearing?"

"Oh, honey. Come with me. I think I've got a pair of Rey's pants that will fit you."

I grabbed him by the waistband of his khakis and dragged him to the bedroom. "Why do you have a pair of Rey's pants?" he asked.

"He stayed with me for a couple of nights when he was having the bedrooms of his brownstone renovated, and he left a few things behind. I keep meaning to return them, but I forget, and Rey probably owns seventeen pairs of black pants, so he never remembers to take them, either. I don't know why I hang on to them. It's not like I can wear them. Rey's wider and shorter than I am."

Jonathan didn't say anything, just stood where I left him near the bed. I started pulling things out of my closet, trying to find Rey's pants, and I dumped random things on the bed. "Oh, here, you should wear this shirt," I said, tossing a green button-down at Jonathan. It had short sleeves and silver pinstripes and was definitely not Jonathan's usual fare, but I thought it would look good on him.

"I can't wear this," he said.

"Why, too small?"

He looked at the size tag. I was a bit thinner than he was, but the shirt was big on me, and I thought it would fit him. "No, it'll probably fit," he said, "but it's not really my—"

"That shade of green would go great with your eyes." I slid hangers along the rack in my closet, trying to decide what I should wear. I extracted a few shirts and held them up. I couldn't decide. "What do you think? Black or red?"

"Black," Jonathan said.

"You're right. This red always makes me look flushed. I don't know why I own this."

I tossed a few more things on the bed and then pulled my T-shirt off over my head, preparing to change. I heard Jonathan's breath catch in his throat. I tossed my T-shirt on the floor and smiled at him. "I heard that. Admiring the merchandise?" I asked. I flexed for good measure.

"Yeah."

This man, I swear. I stepped toward him. He stood there, holding the shirt I had given him. I put my hands on either side of his face and kissed him. I loved kissing him. The way our lips fit together gave me such a charge. I felt like all of my blood was running south, which I suspect was actually the case since I got hard. Just from kissing him.

"Hold that thought," I said as I pulled away. I spotted Rey's pants on the bed and tossed them at Jonathan. "Put those clothes on."

"I can't go out with you," he said.

I pulled off my jeans and looked at him like he wasn't fooling anybody. "What are you afraid of?"

I stood there in only a pair of briefs, and I was sure my erection was obvious, but Jonathan wasn't looking at me. He looked at the floor and rolled up the clothes in his hands. "It's one thing to spend time with you here, but to go out in public? And dancing? I'm a terrible dancer. And I'm not... what if someone recognizes me? I mean, there was a big picture of me next to your article, and a few more have popped up in the paper since, and all I need is the wrong person to blab, and if my father found out...."

"Come on. We put you in those clothes and some eyeliner, wash that gel out of your hair, no one will recognize you."

"Eyeliner? I'm not wearing makeup."

That was a damn shame. "You'd look hot in eyeliner."

"Drew...."

I laughed, trying to lighten the mood, trying to infect him with my good mood. "Fine, no eyeliner. Come on, we'll go to one of my favorite clubs. I know the people there. You have nothing to worry about."

Jonathan looked down at the clothes in his hand. He nodded.

I didn't like feeling like I'd pressured him into this, but I knew I had. I justified it by telling myself this would be good for him. I pushed him into the bathroom and turned on the water in the shower. "Strip," I ordered.

He complied. We fooled around a little in the shower, but I was of singular purpose, and I carefully washed Jonathan's hair. He closed his eyes and let me do what I wanted. I washed my own hair while Jonathan just stood there watching. He was hard too. I wanted to touch him, but I didn't want to waste any time. We'd have sex later. That, and I liked the idea of us letting the desire we had for each other build over the course of a night until we couldn't hold ourselves back any longer. I pulled him back out of the shower and toweled us both dry.

I saw that Jonathan was so nervous he couldn't get his breathing under control, but every time I asked if he was really okay, he told me he was. He put on the clothes I had given him, the green shirt and Rey's black pants. I spent some time trying in vain to tame my wild hair. When we were both ready, I grabbed Jonathan's hand. We flew out of my building and out onto the street.

"How'd you get here?" I asked when we hit the sidewalk.

"Car service," Jonathan admitted, pulling his hand out of mine.

"Let's take the subway."

Which was how we came to be standing outside of a club in the Village called Rooster's half an hour later. "They're not even trying to be subtle, are they?" Jonathan asked.

"When I was in college, I frequented a place called Manhole."

He laughed. "Okay, that's worse." But he dug in his heels when I tried to pull him inside.

"Jonathan, no one's going to recognize you."

And still he hesitated. "I can't be here. Going with you to a restaurant or a bar would be one thing, but this is, you know, a club where, you know…." He pressed his palms together.

"Are you trying to say that this is a homosexual establishment?" I clutched at my invisible pearls. "Rey's gone in here with me before, and he's a hell of a lot higher profile than you are. In the unlikely event someone does recognize you, well, it's not totally unprecedented for the straight friends of gay men to go to gay clubs. Because you know what else they have at gay clubs? Straight-girl best friends."

"I'm not here to pick up women," Jonathan said.

"I should hope not." I leaned close to him. "I'm just concocting your alibi. Do you see anybody you think you might be here to pick up?"

I could see it on his face when he started to let go. The lines in his forehead disappeared; his mouth twitched into an almost smile. "I think I might see someone," he said, looking right at me.

"Yeah?" I laughed, and Jonathan laughed with me. That seemed like a green light. "Let's go inside. Deep breath, cowboy."

I held out my hand for him, and he took it. We walked into the club together. Once we were inside, everything was loud music and lights flashing. Jonathan had a deer-in-the-headlights expression on his face. A song I liked started to play.

"Let's dance," I said. "This is a great song."

I gestured toward the dance floor. There was a sea of dancers that looked like a heaving mass of human flesh, not distinct people. It was the sort of crowd one could get lost in.

"I'm not much of a dancer," he said. "I think I'll just go get a drink. Do you want anything?"

"Gin and tonic. Oh, I see someone I know. I'll meet you at the bar in a few minutes."

Jonathan tapped my wrist with his fingers before moving towards the bar. I wasn't sure what the gesture meant, but it felt a little bit like a good-bye.

I opted not to dwell. I'd spotted Rob dancing by himself in the crowd, so I sidled up to him. When he saw me, he squealed and threw his arms around me, so I returned the hug, and it probably lasted longer than was appropriate, but man, I had missed this. I missed my friends. I missed feeling the throb of the music in my chest; I missed being mashed together with all these other men; I missed everyone's infectious enthusiasm. Rob put his hands on my hips, and we danced together for a minute. Then he leaned close and said, "Is your new man here?"

I nodded. "He went to get a drink."

He grinned. "I want to meet him."

"Come find us at the bar later."

I gave Rob a brief kiss on the lips before pulling away. His husband, Hal, appeared then and snaked his arms around Rob from behind. Our eyes met and we nodded to acknowledge each other. It was too loud to speak.

The song switched to something mellower, so I excused myself and went to find Jonathan. There was an empty stool next to him at the bar, so I slid onto it and took a sip of the gin and tonic waiting for me.

"Friend of yours?" Jonathan asked, pointing back toward the mob.

I swung around so that my back was leaning against the bar. I propped my elbows on it and looked out at the dancers. "You jealous?"

"No."

His ears burned red with the lie. "You are, so I'll tell you that the man I was dancing with is my friend Rob, who is married to the blond guy he's making out with now." I waited for Jonathan to find him in the crowd. Rob and Hal were kissing like they were trying to climb into each other's mouths. Ah, love. "I've known Rob since college, but we never dated or anything. He *is* just a friend."

"Okay," said Jonathan. He scanned the room. I wondered if maybe he was looking for someone he knew, or, more accurately, someone who might recognize him. As far as I could tell, no one was paying us any mind.

"Andrew, darling!" a voice called. I looked up and saw my old friend Miss Darla coming toward us. She pulled me into a fierce hug before I could summon a reaction. "It's been so long, how are you!"

"I'm fantastic, Miss Darla. How are you?"

She straightened up and grinned. "Fabulous as always. Who's your cute friend?"

Miss Darla raised an eyebrow at Jonathan. His gaze was on her Adam's apple. There was an evident struggle on his face as he suppressed a grin.

"Jonathan, Darla, Darla, Jonathan," I said.

"Nice to meet you," Jonathan said.

Miss Darla smiled politely. "Andrew and I go way back," she said.

"Yeah?"

"I had a roommate in college who did drag on the weekends," I said. "He talked me into writing an article for the college paper on this amateur contest they used to hold at a club in Chelsea. My roommate entered, and Miss Darla here took him under her wing."

"Andrew and I have been friends ever since," said Miss Darla. She turned back to me. "It's great to see you out and about and looking so happy."

"Thanks." It was like I'd been gravely ill. My behavior for the last few months suddenly seemed very silly.

"You know, your boy from Boston is here."

I put some effort into not letting my smile fade and probably was not entirely successful. Because, of course, I was panicking. "Aaron," I said. I'd told Jonathan that particular sob story the week before. I caught him flinching out of the corner of my eye. To Darla, I said, "How does he look? How is he?"

"Same as always. Too charming for his own good."

I shrugged. "Whatever. I'm over it."

"Are you?"

"Yeah." I meant it this time. "I mean, I cried for three days after he left, but time has given me some perspective. Aaron is a great guy, but I have come to realize that we had some fundamental incompatibilities."

"I'll say!" Miss Darla guffawed. "Like the fact that you're both tops."

Jonathan blushed, which I thought was cute. Besides, the top thing had been the least of our problems; Aaron and I had always had a good and imaginative sex life.

I laughed with Darla. "Actually, I was going to say that we had differing definitions of monogamy. My definition said that we should sleep with only each other, but his said he should sleep with many other men, as often as possible. I confronted him about this and *he* had the nerve to dump *me*."

"Oh, Andrew," said Miss Darla, laughing. "I always tell that man that he didn't appreciate what he had in you. You stay marvelous, okay?"

"I will try, Darla."

Miss Darla turned back to Jonathan and dropped her voice. "You don't break his heart, okay? Because Miss Darla will come after you if you do." She grinned, but there was a little bit of malice in that smile.

And then who should appear but the man himself. Aaron waltzed up to the bar, casual as you please. "Drew," he said. He made eye contact with the bartender, who immediately got to work making him a martini.

He looked good, which made me angry. He had on a black wife beater and a pair of snug jeans, and he stood there insouciantly with all his strawberry blond and freckly good looks. The bartender slid his martini in front of him. He picked out the olive and popped it in his mouth.

"Aaron. How are you?" I asked. I was aware of Jonathan standing behind me, but I had to deal with this situation one problem at a time.

Aaron grinned. "I'm fine. Haven't seen *you* in a while."

"I've been busy."

Aaron ran a hand through his hair. "Sure you have."

It's an interesting experience, getting your heart sliced open with a crowd of onlookers. Aaron looked as cool and calm as always, sipping his martini and eyeing me. I had this flash of our whole relationship. We'd been happy for a large part of the time we were together. Aaron was a lot of fun. But I had bigger dreams than just fun. I wanted to be in love. I wanted to start a family. I wanted someone willing to commit to me. Was that so much to ask?

I felt a hand on my back. *Jonathan.*

"He's been busy with me," Jonathan said.

His voice was like a needle scratching across a record. I needed a moment to process that Jonathan was coming to my rescue. Then something in me snapped. "I suppose," I said to Aaron, "that you expected me to stay at home, moping and crying over you."

"I never said that." He sipped from his martini again. "Look, I'm sorry if I hurt you—"

"Who says you did?"

Aaron raised an eyebrow. "Come on, Drew."

"Okay, I was upset when you left, but it was, what, seven months ago?" That hand on my back snuck around my waist possessively, and it did not escape Aaron's notice. He stared at the hand. "I've moved on," I said.

"I wanted us to be friends, you know. You're the one who went all drama queen on me."

"If he stopped talking to you, I'm guessing he had a good reason." Jonathan propped his chin on my shoulder. I could feel his chest press into my back. His presence was helping ease my anxiety a little. He must have noticed that my heart was racing and kept picking up momentum as the conversation progressed. Jonathan added, "And I know we just met, but I can already tell he's better off without you."

Aaron glanced at Darla. "Is this guy for real?"

Time to put an end to this, I decided. "I don't think…," I started to say, but I had to stop and gather my thoughts. I took a deep breath. "We can't be friends, Aaron. Too much damage. And I'm not having this argument here. What I'm going to do is have another drink and make out with my date. I'm sure there are dozens of guys here who would happily blow you in the bathroom, since that's the greatest amount of intimacy you are capable of."

He ground his teeth. At length he said, "Whatever." He downed the rest of his martini and flounced off.

Darla hooted. "Oh, lord, that was something."

It was about then that I started shaking. Saying all that to Aaron, forcing him to go away, had taken a significant effort on my part.

Jonathan pressed his nose into my shoulder, which I found comforting. He moved so his lips were near my ear. "So that was him?"

"The infamous Aaron in the flesh."

"He's hot," Jonathan said.

"Yeah." I couldn't deny it. "But he's reckless."

"He's been worse since you broke up," Darla said under her breath. "Goes home with whoever will take him. And a man who looks like Aaron, he could have anyone here, except for that funky smell of desperation. I'd say you were not the only one who got his heart stomped on when your relationship ended."

I took a deep breath. "You know what? Fuck him."

"Fuck who?"

I looked up and saw Rob and Hal approach. Here was a new layer of anxiety on top of the churning in my stomach. Bad enough introducing your new boyfriend to your old one; now he had to meet my friends. It occurred to me that there was also the legitimate fear that Rob and Hal, as devoted readers of my column, would recognize him. I was pretty sure they could keep a secret, but if they *did* recognize him, that would surely freak Jonathan right out. I pushed my glass away, worried I'd vomit. Darla patted my head and ordered me a glass of water.

"Was that Aaron I just saw?" Hal asked.

"Yep," I said.

Jonathan's arm was still around me, his chest still pressed into my back. I closed my eyes for a moment and leaned into him. I hoped to convey telepathically that I appreciated him being there with me. I don't know if he got that or not. He kissed my shoulder and then eased away when I introduced him to Hal and Rob as just "Jonathan," praying they wouldn't recognize his resemblance to my recent interview subject. They all shook hands. Rob and Hal, thankfully, seemed oblivious.

Hal asked about where Jonathan lived, which led them into a convoluted conversation about new restaurants in Boerum Hill. (Hal was a foodie and occasional restaurant critic.) Rob pulled me aside slightly. Darla bowed her head to participate in the conversation also.

"Nicely done," Rob said. "He's really cute."

"Thanks," I said. "I really like him."

"I can see that," said Darla. "And the way he got all touchy when Aaron showed up! Good for him!"

"How did that go?" asked Rob.

"Eh," I said. "It's well and truly over. Aaron's being petulant. And I'm with Jonathan now. So, as I said, fuck him."

Rob rubbed my arm affectionately.

My water appeared, so I took a long sip. There was small talk between everyone and Jonathan, so I leaned back and watched. I started to calm down somewhat.

The song changed again to one of my favorites, and I sat up. I slid off the stool and stood next to Jonathan. I grabbed his arm. "Oh, I love this song! Come on, dance with me!"

"I'm really not a good dancer," Jonathan said.

"I don't care. Please? Come on! What is the point of coming here tonight if we're not going to dance?"

"Better do what he wants," Darla advised. "I'll keep your stool warm."

Jonathan reluctantly let me take his hand and drag him over to the crowd of dancers. Then he abruptly stopped walking right before we got to the floor.

"What?" I asked.

He looked around. "Are you really okay? With what happened with Aaron."

"Yes. Better than ever."

"Just making sure."

He was so endearingly cute, his brow furrowed with concern for me.

I said, "Thanks for stepping in there. I think if you hadn't been with me, I would have, I don't know. Crumbled. Let him win. Which, trust me, he does not deserve."

"Fuck him." Jonathan leaned close. "You are so sexy. I'm not the only one who thinks so, because I've been watching other guys check you out all night. Including Aaron. He was definitely jealous."

Hmm, this was interesting. I smiled. "Well, if I learned nothing else from my relationship with him, it's that there's a hell of a lot more to making something work than two pretty people coming together. Two people hooking up? That's just fucking. I want so much more than that."

"Yeah," he said, though he seemed to have gone into some kind of lust-filled fugue state, because he was staring at my mouth and his hand had snaked under my shirt to rest on the bare skin of my side.

I wasn't sure if he was listening anymore, but I took a risk. "There's something to be said for hooking up with a hot guy, but I want a lot more than that, and I want it with *you.*"

He nodded slowly. He looked up and our eyes met. He opened his mouth to speak.

But, feeling embarrassed now, I cut him off. "Thus ends this topic and all discussion of Aaron. Now we are dancing."

I pulled him into the crowd. I let go once we were ensconced in the midst of the horde, and I started dancing happily. I'm not an especially good dancer, either, but that was beside the point. I always thought the real joy of dancing in a gay club was being in that room full of sweaty men, everyone moving and dancing and sexually charged. Plenty of naked male chest was on display. Couples were forming and breaking up and making out all around us. It was hard not to get caught up in the energy of the crowd, in the smell of sweat and sex and man. It got my blood pumping, that was for sure.

Jonathan clearly had no sense of rhythm, and I watched him try to make his body move with the music, a little awkwardly at first, but he kind of just gave in as the song went on. The music had a metronomic beat over which a man with a thin voice sang. It was a love song. I sang along with the lyrics. I sang the song to Jonathan.

His continued attempts at dancing were adorable. So, yes, he was a terrible dancer. But as he slowly lost his inhibitions, there was something erotic about his moves, too, the way he wiggled his hips and swung his arms around. Plus, he looked really good in the shirt I'd loaned him; I was inclined to let him keep it. When I smiled at him, he reached out an arm and put it on my shoulder, which was all the encouragement I needed to grab his waist and pull him close, pressing our bodies together. He sighed and put his arms around my neck. I kept on singing and bent my head to press my forehead against his. I ground my hips against his suggestively and could feel his erection pressing against me. I was so turned on I wanted to rip his clothes off right there in the middle of the dance floor. Instead, I snuck a hand up inside his shirt and pressed it against the warm skin of his back.

Then the beat picked up and it clicked in my head that we were in a mass of other people who, granted, were in various states of undress, but I figured it was better not to scare Jonathan too much. I pushed away and went back to dancing. Jonathan panted and he was sweaty enough that the fringe of hair that fell in his face was damp, but he looked happy. He laughed and started aping my movements, and he looked a little ridiculous but also incredibly sexy.

So I kissed him. He responded eagerly, snaking his arms back around my neck, his hands up into my hair. He tasted of whiskey and he was sweaty, his skin clammy, but I loved how he smelled. I could feel his heart pounding against my chest. I pulled away slightly, but he pulled me back, kissing me again.

The song ended, and I pulled him off the dance floor again. The volume of the music near the bar was somewhat less deafening, so I pulled him back over near it so we could hear each other speak.

"Thank you for coming out with me tonight," I said. "I know this is way outside your comfort zone."

"You know what? I'm having a good time."

"Good."

"And it so happens that I've snagged this amazing man."

"Ooh, tell me more."

"He's totally hot. He has this cute little dimple in his left cheek, even. And he's really tall and has a great body too."

"Aw, shucks."

"And he makes me laugh and he takes me dancing and I'm doing all these things with him that I've never done before, that I was always afraid to do, but it's great, I'm having a great time with him."

"He sounds like a great guy."

"He is. You'd like him."

I laughed. "You know, I met a guy about a month ago. He's got some issues, but he's totally hot, too, with these amazing green eyes."

"Yeah?" Jonathan said.

"Being out with you tonight, I feel more alive than I have in months." And that was the honest truth. Aaron's leaving had put me into some kind of catatonic state, but I'd faced him without crumbling and, more to the point, here I was, out with Jonathan. All that time I'd lost mourning Aaron seemed wasted.

Jonathan looked puzzled, his eyebrows pressed together, like he was trying to figure out what to say.

"Don't say anything," I said. "Just dance with me. Just keep dancing."

So that's what we did.

CHAPTER
Twelve

I HUMMED to myself as I walked into my kitchen. I couldn't remember a time when I'd felt so good. Jonathan had gone out with me, which I knew had been a lot to push him into doing, but he'd come through it happy and laughing. We'd come back to my place and made love slowly, well into the night. We woke up together, which felt pretty great. Now it was morning and the sun was streaming through the kitchen window. I could hear birds chirping.

Jonathan was parked on the couch with my laptop propped in his lap. As I got the coffee going, I heard him say, "Fuck."

I popped my head out of the kitchen and looked at him. He changed his tune to, "Oh shit, oh shit, oh shit."

"What is it?" I asked.

Reading from the laptop's screen, Jonathan said, "'Blind item: which über-conservative politician's son was seen outside gay club Rooster's last night, hand-in-hand with a cute taller man?'"

"Aw, they think I'm cute."

"Drew, this is a big problem. Someone recognized me."

"So? The blind item is pretty vague. It doesn't even specify what office the politician holds. Could be any conservative politician. I can think of a dozen off-hand who have sons in their twenties."

Jonathan closed the laptop and put it on the coffee table. "My father read that. He's going to call any minute." His phone rang. "See? Fuck."

"Come on, it'll be fine."

"Here, I'll put it on speaker so you can understand what I have to deal with." He pushed a few buttons on his phone, then answered it, "Hi, Dad."

"Tell me it wasn't you outside of a gay club."

It was completely fucking surreal to hear the Senator's voice through the phone. I thought about what Rey had said when he'd reminded me that Richard Granger was a real person with a family and all that. I knew, of course, that Jonathan was the son of this man whom I'd spent so much energy hating, but I don't think I really understood until the moment Senator Granger's voice came booming through Jonathan's phone.

Jonathan said, "It's great to hear from you, too, Dad. How are you?"

I sat on the coffee table, my knees touching his. I put a hand on his thigh in an attempt to be comforting.

"We talked about this, Jonny. When you went to New York, this was not the sort of publicity you were expected to get." Man, that voice. I'd heard it on TV, giving speeches, informing me and other people like me that we'd rot in hell while he stood superior on the other side of a podium. I *hated* that voice. It was patronizing and condescending and offensive. That the voice belonged to Jonathan's father—and, let's face it, I was completely gone over Jonathan—didn't endear him to me at all.

Jonathan remained relatively stoic. He said, "It's a vague blind item. It could be about the president's son for all we know. Senator Kent has a son about my age who lives in New York City, as does the mayor of Albany."

There was a hissing sound as Jonathan's father sighed into the phone. "All right. Fine. How are you, Jonny?"

"I'm okay."

"How's work?"

This had just taken a strange turn. I listened to Jonathan and his father relate mundane news to each other: Jonathan's job was going well, one of his students had won some kind of city-wide science award; Richard and his wife had just booked a vacation in Aspen in March; the Senator had been really busy with work for the Armed Services Committee. Well, that last bit was maybe less mundane, but he apologized to Jonathan for not calling much lately. He finished by saying, "I'm glad things are going well. I apologize for overreacting."

"Let me ask you something," Jonathan said. He looked me right in the eyes. I sensed that he was about to do something daring. I wasn't sure if I was proud or scared.

"I have a meeting in forty-five minutes," said the Senator. "I hate to cut you off, but I need you to make it quick."

"Just hypothetically, what if it were me? In the blind item, I mean."

"It wouldn't be. You wouldn't be that stupid."

And there it was. I was about ready to forgive the Senator, but then he reminded me why I didn't like him. Jonathan held my gaze and said, "But say it was. Hypothetically. Say I went to a gay club and was seen there. How would you react?"

There was a long pause before Senator Granger answered, "Well, I guess we could explain it away. You were there with a friend. I don't approve of the lifestyle of those people, but maybe you went there to meet a woman, yeah? Or you were mistaken about the, uh, nature of the club."

I mouthed, *Those people?* It was like a punch in the gut. It was difficult enough to reconcile the guy on the phone with Senator Granger's public persona, given how nice he was being to Jonathan. He was starting to win me over—or at least I began to doubt that he felt as vehemently about his opinions in private as he expressed in public—but "those people"? That hurt.

A siren wailed outside and I stifled a sneeze, but that was apparently enough to alert the Senator that Jonathan was not nestled in his quiet apartment. "Where are you?" his father asked.

"A friend's. Let me ask you something else." Jonathan was really getting into it now. "What would you do if I were one of 'those people'?"

"This is ridiculous, Jonny. I have to get to my meeting. You are not—"

"But what if I was? What if I walked outside right now and said, 'I'm a gay man!' for all of New York to hear. What would you do?"

"We've talked about this. You said it was a phase you went through in college." Uncertainty crept into the Senator's voice. "Besides, you promised you wouldn't—"

"But what if I did? I'm an adult, I go to clubs sometimes, and I have gay friends. If I went to a club with a friend and someone saw me there, it could start a bunch of rumors even if it weren't true. What if someone connected the rumor to your campaign? Or what if I told someone I was gay and it got out? What if I came out publicly in a magazine article or on a website? You can't disown me. Too much negative publicity. Doesn't do much for your 'family values' image."

"Nothing would happen, because you will do no such thing. Come out publicly?"

"I'm not asking for your permission."

I gasped. I didn't realize I was about to speak until Jonathan held his hand up and touched my lips.

There was another long pause on the other end of the phone line. "What are you saying?" asked the Senator.

"What if, Dad, what if I did go to that club last night, huh? What if I went there with my boyfriend? What if we came back to his place afterwards and the doorman saw us? What if I spent the night? What if I'm still there?"

Boyfriend was the word that stuck in my head. "Guy I fuck sometimes" was what I expected he thought of me. "Lover" would have been okay. But "boyfriend"? This conversation was about to take a turn for the worse, I could sense it, and Jonathan was speaking hypothetically—I didn't have a doorman. Still, I was ashamed to find such joy in such a silly word. Boyfriend. I could hardly believe it.

"You stop that right now," the Senator said. "I will not listen to nonsense like this from you. You know what I'd do? I'd move you back to Washington where I could keep an eye on you. This is not the time for experimenting, son. I'm running for national office, and I can't have any scandal attached to the campaign."

Of course. Being gay was a scandal. I wondered if the actual fact of Jonathan's homosexuality—which Richard Granger must have seen in his son, had probably known about for years—didn't matter as much as public perception. Granger had a conservative base to appease. It was hard to tell, though. If the circumstances were different, if Richard Granger were just a guy with an office job instead of a public figure, would he be this stubborn? Would he be able to accept his son?

Jonathan was growing visibly frustrated. He kept running his free hand through his hair, and his skin was flushed. "You can't seriously think that moving me to Washington is going to solve anything. And forcing me to move would just get you more publicity."

"I have never known you to be so… insubordinate. I can't publicly disown you, but I can cut you off. You want money to live off of? You will do as I say. I don't want to hear any more about this phase you seem to fancy yourself going through. You are not gay. You are my son and you are not gay." The Senator's voice cracked as he said the last sentence, but Jonathan didn't seem to notice.

In fact, his face was twisted up with some kind of defiant anger. "I'm not moving," he said with conviction.

"You will do as I say." The authority in the Senator's voice reminded me of why he was considered a formidable political opponent, a powerful man, the sort of man who was considered a viable candidate to be leader of the free world. I couldn't imagine having a man like that for a father. This was a man not used to losing.

And, as one might have expected in the face of that authority, all the fight drained out of Jonathan. "But...."

"What happened to that nice teacher you were dating?"

"We weren't even really dating. I told you, we went on that one date, and it didn't go that well—"

"Try her again. That's where your future lies."

"Dad, I—"

"I appreciate that you're going through a rough time. So things didn't work out with the teacher. There are plenty of other women in New York. Your striking out with one does not make you gay. Do not persist with this nonsense. I don't have time for it. I have a campaign to run. You know that this is hardly the time to stir up trouble. You must do nothing to risk the campaign. If you do, that's it. Do I need to remind you that I pay for that apartment you live in?"

Jonathan's face crumbled. My heart went out to him. I was secure in my sexuality and as out as it got, and I think I would have caved in to the Senator too. "No. Please, Dad. I was kidding. It's... fine. I won't do anything or say anything. Please. I want to stay in New York."

"I don't want to hear any more nonsense from you about being one of... those."

"No, nothing, I swear."

"Good, because the next item like this I see, you're done. I'm cutting you off."

"I understand."

"All right. I hate to take this rough stance, but I can't risk the campaign. I've worked too hard. You know how hard I've worked. Your mother's out, but I'll have her call you later."

"That's fine."

"Bye, son."

Jonathan hung up the phone. He stared at it for a long time and then dropped it, his hands shaking. I reached out for him. He hesitated at first, but I persisted and pulled him into my arms.

"You see what I'm up against?" Jonathan whispered.

"I'm so sorry." What a mess. I had no idea how to make this better. It had started to feel like Jonathan was coming into his own, that, even if he didn't end up with me, he could find a way to be happy with himself. I wanted that for him more than anything.

And I wanted to be with him. I thought, as I stroked his hair and held his shaking body, that maybe I could pretend publicly that he and I were just friends if it meant I got to be with him in private. Of course, my resentment towards his father would only fester and grow, and I knew that, too, and I just could not think of a way out of that bind. Would the specter of Richard Granger always poison our relationship? Could I overcome that? Should I have to? I considered the cost to Jonathan. He could defy his father, but I realized that doing so would mean not only getting cut off financially but probably getting cut off from his whole family. He didn't deserve that.

Jonathan sniffed. "I want to do what's right. But he controls me. Even if he didn't, I don't know if I'm ready to come out, but maybe I could... but the way he is, how can I? What the hell am I supposed to do?"

"You get by however you can," I said. "I don't know. You save up so you don't need your father's money. You get your own place in New York that your father doesn't pay for. You hang onto the people who love you for who you really are. You just... live your life."

"How can he do this to me?"

I touched the side of Jonathan's face and realized he was crying. I felt that deeply and wished more than anything that I could come up with an easy solution. I realized that Jonathan's pain came more from his inability to gain his father's acceptance than anything else. I wiped the tears from his cheek with my thumb and kissed the top of his head. "I'm so sorry, J. I really am. I can't imagine how hard this must be for you. If you want to lay low for a while, I understand."

"I don't want to lay low. What I really want is to tell my dad to fuck off."

"An admirable goal. I have often wanted to tell your dad to fuck off."

Jonathan pulled away and looked at me, frowning. "I had so much fun last night. I like spending time with you. I don't want my father to take that away from me. He has no right."

"So don't let him control you."

"Easier said than done. And I don't know if I can do all this. Go out with you, be with you in public. I know you want that, but I'm not sure I... How can I... I mean, is this really what I want?" He sighed and pressed his face into my shoulder. He inhaled deeply. "I want to be with you, just like this. And this is pretty much all I have to give."

"I disagree. I think you have a lot to give." I stroked his back. "But I know. I get it." I hated the Senator more than ever then, for making Jonathan choose between his true self and his family. Or, let's face it, Richard Granger was trying to make Jonathan choose between me and his family, and that was really not fair. "I can be patient. Seeing you stand up to your father just now, I know how hard that must have been for you."

"Yeah. You've already been so patient."

I laughed softly in an effort to lighten the mood. I held Jonathan and gave his shoulders a squeeze. "Despite my better judgment, I like you a lot. I like spending time with you too. Look, I know this is hard. It can take time. You think I didn't shit a wall's worth of bricks before I came out to my mother? And Mom is totally cool with everything. She's never been anything but supportive of me. I think I could have told her I wanted to have sex with a rhinoceros and she would have hugged me and told me she loved me no matter what. And still I fretted over it. This thing with your dad must be a thousand times worse. What you just did was really brave. So take all the time you need."

"I don't deserve you," he said.

"Probably not."

Jonathan pulled away slightly and lifted his head up. He kissed me so sweetly my heart ached. Then he whispered, "Take me to bed. Make love to me. I need you right now."

"Are you sure?"

"Yes. Please?"

I stood and let Jonathan lead me back to the bedroom.

Without a word, Jonathan undressed and then undressed me. He looked at me, his gaze traveling from my chest, across my collarbone, then up to my face. Our eyes met and I could see all of the anguish in his, his shame and his pain and the untenable position he'd been put in. He leaned up and kissed me. I pulled him into my arms and pressed our bodies together, holding him tightly as we stood at the foot of my bed. I wanted him and I wanted for this to be okay and I wanted for him to be happy.

He pulled away, then sat on the bed. He grabbed my arms and pulled me down with him. I straddled him. He leaned up and kissed me again. Then he kissed my cheek, my jaw, my neck. He whispered my name. His breath was hot against my skin. I tangled my fingers in his hair, and he licked and bit me aggressively, his teeth scraping against my chest.

I couldn't have stopped us if I'd wanted to. My body bent towards his as he slowly devoured me. I didn't just want him, I needed him. I needed to feel that physical connection to him, I needed to be inside him, I needed him around me. I ran my hands across his shoulders and felt his smooth skin, so familiar to me now. I knew where that birthmark on his back was, knew where each of his scars was, knew how each of his imperfections came together to make one perfect whole, and I wanted to be a part of it, to be a part of him.

I gently pushed him back onto the bed so that he was lying flat on his back. I ran my hands down his chest, grazing my palms over the hairs there, over his nipples, over his abs. I guessed, based on the way his back curved like a bow off the bed, on the way his hard red cock rested on his belly, that he needed me just as badly as I needed him. I grabbed what I needed from the bedside drawer, and then I dove, tasting the skin of his chest, licking and kissing the long line of his torso, the curve of his hip, the base of his cock. I took him into my mouth as I prepared him for our coupling, as I pressed my fingers inside him and felt the beginnings of that connection. This was not merely about sensation or about getting off anymore, but about something bigger than each of us.

He keened and moaned, grasping at my hair as my tongue traveled the length of his cock. He whispered my name again, then started to repeat it over and over again. Then he yanked on my hair hard enough that it hurt. I let go of his cock and looked up at him to figure out what he was doing. He moved quickly and kissed me, then pushed me onto my back. He rolled the condom on me, then straddled my hips. Before I could react, he was sinking onto me and I was at long last sliding inside him.

I groaned as I felt that tightness. He closed his eyes tightly for a moment, but I could see it the second things eased from the initial pain into something far more pleasurable. He propped his hands on my chest and began to move, controlling the pace. All sensation seemed concentrated in that place where our bodies met, as his body surrounded and squeezed me. I wanted to touch him everywhere. I ran my hands all over every bit of skin I could, over his shoulders, down his arms, across his chest. I wrapped a hand around his cock and stroked it as he slid on and off me. He was so beautiful, the way his back arched away, the way his lips parted, the way his Adam's apple bobbed in the long column of his throat as he sighed and moaned.

I wanted us to be closer, so I pushed my knees up, then pulled him down so that my arms were around him and our chests touched. I felt his heart beating, could feel that irregular pulse moving through his body. I pushed inside him, sliding in and out, letting those sensations travel the length of me, the length of my cock and of my whole body, electrical pulses making my skin feel alive. He kissed me and pushed against me over and over. Then he groaned and I felt his cock jerk in my hand just before he came between us. I managed to roll us over so that I was on top again without leaving his body, without breaking that connection, and I felt like I was fighting against the tide of my own orgasm, building with aching slowness until I was half desperate and crying out his name and finally coming inside him.

LATER, I lay on top of him, feeling thoroughly spent and slightly uncomfortable but liking how our bodies pressed together. He sighed and put his arms around my shoulders.

"Were you just speaking hypothetically earlier when you referred to me as your boyfriend?" I asked. The question had been nagging at me since the capacity for rational thought had returned post-orgasm.

I propped myself up on my elbows so that I could look down at him. His nose was scrunched up in an exaggerated way, like maybe he was having trouble making his brain recollect things that had happened further back than the last half hour. "Uh, when I was talking to my father?"

"Yeah."

"I don't know. I think so. Or not." He kneaded at my shoulder muscles. "I guess I kind of think of you as my boyfriend."

"I want to be your boyfriend."

"That's good."

I shifted slightly and pressed my cheek against Jonathan's. I whispered in his ear, "You know what else I want?"

"What?"

"I want to take you out every night too. I want to be outside where the lights are bright and hold your hand and kiss you in public." I sighed. "I want everything with you." And that was a pretty scary truth. Given what a mess my break up with Aaron had left me, it was terrifying to get involved with someone again so soon. And even then, the stakes were so much higher here, the odds of it ending badly really high.

I felt dampness against my cheek and knew he was crying again. I figured he wouldn't want me to acknowledge it, so I didn't really react besides to hold him tighter. We stayed quiet for a long time. Eventually, he sniffed.

"I'm sorry," he said.

"It's okay, J."

"What if I can never give you what you want?"

"You can. You will."

"My father. The public. My family. I don't know if I can risk...."

I tried to be optimistic. He had to overcome a mountain of his own issues before we'd ever really be okay, but I thought maybe after the campaign—after the Senator was not so much in the spotlight, when Jonathan might have the privacy and time he needed to reconcile where he came from and who he was and who he wanted to be—things between us could be really great. I said, "I can be patient."

"But what if...?"

"Shh." I kissed him, thus ending the discussion.

CHAPTER
Thirteen

I HAD brunch with Allie and Rey the next day. I wasn't feeling so well, unsure of what to do about Jonathan and kind of emotionally drained.

I'd picked up a copy of the *Post* that someone had abandoned on the subway and carried it in with me. Rey and Allie were already there, seated at a table in the middle of the restaurant and, if their body language was anything to judge by, flirting with each other. I couldn't deal with that, either. I walked to the table, sat down, tossed the paper at Rey, and said, "Maybe I should start with a mimosa. Or, like, a whole bottle of tequila."

"Are you okay?" Allie asked.

I shrugged.

"Man troubles," Rey guessed.

I buried my head in my hands. "I don't want to talk about it." Or, really, I did, but not with Allie, who still didn't know about Jonathan or any of the situation.

Rey seemed to understand. He opened the paper. "Am I looking for something specific, or are you just being charitable?"

I signaled for the waitress. I needed coffee. And booze. "Third page, second column, about halfway down." When the waitress appeared, I ordered coffee and a mimosa, figuring that covered all the bases.

When she left, Rey read the gossip item out loud for Allie's benefit. "'Sexy small-screen star Reynolds Blethwyn has been seen around town with little blond starlet Misha Krantz. Could this be the beginning of a hot coupling?'" Rey grinned. "We went on *one* date, and it becomes 'seen around town with'."

"She was in that movie about the hostage crisis, right?" asked Allie. "She played the president's daughter?"

"That's her all right. She's a real firecracker."

"Are you going to see her again?" I asked.

"Still deciding. I like her and all… but, I mean, I want to keep an open mind." He winked at Allie.

I grabbed the paper and hit him over the head with it. "Seriously? The paper calls you sexy and puts you together with a hot starlet instead of a dude and you're playing the field now?"

Rey shrugged.

I glanced at Allie to see if she was put off by this conversation at all. I hadn't had a chance to talk to her much about Rey's recent revelation that they'd slept together. Really, I wanted to know if she was into him more than she was letting on. She seemed fairly indifferent to Rey's slutty ways. She casually ate a strawberry. Maybe she *had* gotten it out of her system.

"Does this not bother you at all?" I asked her.

"Why would it?" Allie was hard to read sometimes. I couldn't tell if it genuinely didn't bother her or if she just didn't want me to think it did. I opted to let it go.

"Well," I said, turning to Rey, "I guess I can see how the gossip item would be flattering. They called me 'cute'."

I realized I'd said it aloud at the same time that Rey and Allie turned to look at me. "What?" Rey asked.

"Nothing."

"Have you been getting yourself in the tabloids?"

"How would I get into the tabloids?"

"I don't know." Rey took the paper back. "Maybe by continuing to see a certain man."

"What's going on here?" Allie asked.

"Nothing," I said.

"Or something is," Rey said to me, "or rather someone, but he told you not to say anything."

I shrugged.

"Hello? Is someone going to enlighten me?" Allie asked.

"Maybe it really is nothing." Rey opened the paper again and flipped through it. He read silently for a moment, then said, "Hey, Drew, have you been to Rooster's recently?"

Shit. I summoned all of my calm. "Two nights ago. Why?"

"Oh, there's a mention of it in the paper. I was just curious."

"Some young actor wind up there and try to say he didn't know it was a gay club?" Allie asked, chuckling.

"Something like that," said Rey.

That blind item had been popping up all over the Internet, outing "the son of a right-wing politician." I hadn't actually noticed anything in that day's edition of the *Post*, so I braced myself and said, "What does the item say?"

Rey read aloud, "'If the rumor we're hearing is true, it could blow the lid off one politician's campaign. His supposedly straight son was seen at gay club Rooster's locking lips with a mystery man'."

Just when I thought it wasn't possible to feel any worse, I got knocked down another rung. This item meant someone had spotted Jonathan inside Rooster's, or that someone had gone digging after the first item had appeared and found someone else who had seen us kissing. Either way, Jonathan was going to be in some deep shit with his father, and it was all my fault. But would it have been better not to have brought Jonathan to the club at all? I wasn't sure it would have been.

Allie said, "Wouldn't it be funny if it was Senator Granger's son?"

Rey and I both turned to gawk at Allie simultaneously.

"What?" she said. "Oh, I forgot, Rey, he's your cousin. I'm sorry."

"Don't worry about it."

Allie tapped her chin. "Well. Kissing a guy is a lot different than just being seen in a gay club. *Those* items always crack me up. Like the actor or whoever couldn't tell what kind of club it was."

And with that, we had moved on. Bless Allie's ignorance.

Rey turned a page causally. "It seems impossible that anyone wouldn't know Rooster's is a gay club. The only way it could broadcast more is if it just changed its name to 'Men Who Like Cock'."

"Ew, Rey," Allie said, giggling. She turned to me. "You really went to Rooster's? Does this mean you're not avoiding Aaron anymore?"

"Yes, that's what it means." I sighed. "I ran into him there."

"Oh, no!" said Allie. "Is that what you were so upset about?"

"No, actually." I had kind of forgotten all about Aaron in the previous twenty-four hours. "You know, I had put him out of my mind until I saw him again. Can you believe that? I wish I could go back in time six months to tell myself how stupid I was being, that there is indeed life after Aaron." Because, seriously, my problems with Aaron? Drop in the bucket compared to what was going on with Jonathan.

"That's something, I guess," said Allie, looking confused.

I related the conversation I'd had with him, leaving out the part about being at the club with Jonathan but including what Miss Darla had said about Aaron acting desperate.

Rey frowned. "That guy's an asshole."

"Yes, thank you, Rey," I said.

"I'm just saying."

"You meet anyone interesting while you were there?" Allie asked.

I glanced at Rey, hoping he could maybe guide me in answering the question. He almost imperceptibly shook his head. "I met up with Rob and Hal," I said.

"Bah. You really need to get laid, Drew," said Allie.

That made me laugh. "Trust me, I think that's the least of my problems right now."

WHEN I answered my door, one thing was abundantly clear: Jonathan, who stood on the landing, was drunk. Completely, stinking, couldn't walk a straight line if he had to, hosed, plastered, hammered drunk.

"Hello," I said. "Thought you were going out with your college friends tonight."

"I did." He looked down at the stairs behind him. "The front door of your building was open. Is it always open?"

"Yeah, the lock's busted most of the time." This seemed like a good time to remind my landlord to fix it again. A sturdy lock was important to keep vagrants and drunk boyfriends out of the building.

"Can I come in?"

I motioned for him to come in and closed the door behind him. I wasn't pleased that he was so drunk, but I decided my night had just gotten a lot more entertaining. I pulled him into my arms. "Can't say I'm sad to see you. What brings you to my corner of Brooklyn?"

He sighed and pressed his palms into my back. "My dad called this afternoon."

"Oh."

"He's going to be in New York next week and wants to have dinner with me and the girlfriend he's convinced I must have."

"Yikes."

He pulled himself out of my arms but still stayed close to me. He said, "You probably know by now about that Internet rumor."

"Yeah, I saw the item in the *Post* yesterday." I wasn't sure if I should reach out to him. I dropped my arms to my sides.

He slurred a little as he spoke. "Dad was furious. He was so angry. It would totally blow his mind if I brought you to dinner, wouldn't it? If he knew my boyfriend was the... how did he phrase it? 'Hack liberal columnist for a no-good trash paper'."

"That's charming." Yikes, had the Senator read my article? Of course it made sense for him to have done so, since it was about his son. I don't know why it never entered my mind that he would have. He probably had an assistant or someone that read my column every week. That knowledge made me feel terrible and kind of ashamed for being so unrelenting in my criticism. Here I thought I'd been shouting into the void, but Granger had probably been reading my column for years. I wondered what he must have thought when he saw my byline on that interview with Jonathan.

"Drew." Jonathan grabbed my arms, pulling my attention back to him. "He sent my CV to a bunch of high schools in the DC area. Without even asking me."

I focused back on the matter at hand. "I'm so sorry," I said, feeling impotent as I said it. This whole thing had spun so far out of my control.

"Well, so, the Senator's gonna be in town next week and I have to have dinner with him and he's going to tell me all about how I'm disappointing him and I just don't know if I can face that."

I didn't know what to say.

But he wasn't done talking. "So I went out tonight with the guys. It's homecoming weekend, you know? There's a bar in Hell's Kitchen that does this whole 'Yay Hoyas!' thing and shows the game and all the alumni come, and I saw a bunch of the guys I was friends with in college. All any of them could talk about was women, and oh, Jonny, you should go home with that one over there, and oh, Jonny, that one's really hot, look at her boobs, blah blah. So I got a little drunk. Or kind of a lot drunk? I stayed at the bar until everyone left. I went to get another drink. Then a woman tried to pick me up!"

All of his words and run-on sentences slurred together. I'd never seen him like this. It would have been funny if the motivation for getting drunk hadn't been the problems with his family. I said, "Yeah? Well, you are irresistible."

"Uh-huh. I came here instead." He grinned, which was adorable.

"Very interesting," I said, before leaning down to kiss him. I think all of the blood in his body had been replaced with liquor. Whiskey seemed to be coming out of his pores. "Mmm, you taste like a distillery."

"I had a bit to drink."

"So you said. Just a bit?"

Jonathan shrugged.

I pulled away and took a step back. "So, a woman tried to pick you up at a bar. And then what?"

"I told her she wasn't my type. When she asked me what my type was, I pointed to the hot bartender!" He put his hand to his forehead and guffawed. "I still can't believe I did that."

"Hot bartender?"

"He gave me his number. He had arms like tree trunks!"

Of course he did. "Well, you're just on fire tonight."

"Don't get jealous. I came here to see you."

"I'm flattered, really. I'm amazed you could find your way over here."

"I'm not *that* drunk."

I sighed and moved away from him so I could take a moment to pace around my living room. "You know, this is the second time you've shown up drunk on my doorstep. I hope this isn't a trend."

"What trend?"

I couldn't decide if I was really angry. I can down a few shots with the best of them, but Jonathan was far beyond a healthy drunk. It wasn't hard to guess why. I gave him the simple explanation: "You get drunk then come to me. Good ol' reliable Drew with nothing better to do on a Saturday night." I dropped onto my couch.

He stood in the middle of the room. "I'm... sorry?" His brow furrowed in drunk confusion.

"Sure you are. You could have called. I might have had plans."

"Yes, I'm sorry. I will call next time."

"Next time you get hammered and want to have sex."

"Yes."

He swayed a little on his feet, losing his balance but then reclaiming it. Every time he made an exaggerated movement, I was reminded that he'd gotten so drunk because his father was now actively trying to suppress who he was, although that couldn't have been the whole story. I would have bet he hadn't tried to correct his college friends' false assumption that he wanted to go home with a woman. Did that make me his dirty little secret? I had a vision of all of this crashing and burning. Could we ever make a relationship work? Did I want to?

I groaned. "I should kick you out."

Jonathan walked over to me and crawled onto the couch. He snaked his arms around me. "But you don't want to."

Dammit. "I really don't."

"Fuck me, Drew. I'll totally make it worth your while." He leaned close to me to whisper suggestive things in my ear. And holy mother!

"Well, when you put it like that...."

CHAPTER
Fourteen

I KNEW a lot about dealing with impossible men, fathers in particular.

Rey once did a short stint on Broadway. He was cast in a new play by a Tony Award-winner that had gotten a fair amount of positive buzz. It was a supporting role, but as soon as he told me he was in something in a real Broadway theater (as opposed to the off-off-Broadway stuff he'd been doing), I did a lot of squealing and hopping up and down. I really thought this would be his big break, that he'd finally made it to the big time, and all of those clichés about actors.

Rey procured opening-night tickets for the five people he was closest to: me, his father, his sister, her husband, and the woman he was dating at the time, whose name I bet even he doesn't remember. I wound up sitting next to Rey's father for the main event.

One thing I can say for Sayer Blethwyn: he tried. Rey's part wasn't that big—he played the ambiguously gay younger brother of the protagonist—and there was a lot of, let's say, adult material in the play. I could see Sayer getting embarrassed whenever Rey had a line about anything sexual. Sayer's body language screamed that he was extremely uncomfortable with a lot of the content in the play.

The five of us met up with Rey after the show. "What did you think?" he asked, his eyes wide with expectation.

Rey's sister Nancy hugged him and told him he was great. Her husband and I each shook his hand. Rey's girlfriend kissed him. Then Rey turned to his father.

"Reynolds," said Sayer, "it was certainly interesting."

Rey's face fell. We'd spoken earlier in the day about how nervous Rey was that his father wouldn't like the play, but he'd hoped that the bright lights of Broadway would either distract him or persuade him that his son had done something well. I think there's probably something inside every boy that wants his father to be proud of him. Rey always hoped his father would show that pride outwardly, would clap him on the back and tell him he'd done a good job, would sing his praises. He was often disappointed.

I watched them awkwardly shake hands. They both looked so much alike, with dark hair and blue eyes and broad frames, though Sayer was going gray at his temples. I knew they loved each other. I knew, even, that Sayer was proud of Rey. But Rey was never quite convinced, and neither man was good at expressing emotion, so they both stood there awkwardly fidgeting while we all waited to see if Sayer would say something else about the play.

Eventually, he said in a neutral tone, "You were pretty good."

You would have thought Sayer had just handed Rey a key to a vault full of gold, based on how brightly his face lit up.

The play didn't do that well. It got tremendous reviews— Rey's performance was called out specifically and praised in a few of them—and a Tony nomination for best play, but ticket sales weren't great. The run was cut short, in fact. Rey was heartbroken, but more than anything, he was worried about his father being disappointed in him.

Of course, it was one thing to be a victim to the vagaries of the New York theater-going community. It was another to always feel like you never measured up. Rey's performance was good, as was the play itself, it just wasn't very popular. It wasn't Rey's failure specifically, though I'm sure he felt like it was, and he got cast on *Brooklyn Heights* not long after that anyway. He was petrified when he called his father to say the play was ending, but Sayer was understanding about it. To a point; he added that it might be time for Rey to consider a career change. Such is the nature of impossible fathers.

I'd told my father I was gay over a compulsory dinner out when I was sixteen, something he arranged every so often so that he could pretend he was still a part of my life. It was easier than you'd think to tell him. He was hardly ever around and I didn't like him much, so I didn't care much what he thought. Mom had been nagging me all week about it, telling me that he should know the whole truth about me, that I should tell him at this dinner. Over the main course, I just said, "I'm gay, just so you know" and picked at my food, and he sat there and appraised me.

After a very long pause, he said, "All right." He ate a bite and then shook his head. "You're so young."

"I'm not that young."

"You're sure?"

"Yes, I'm sure. You knew you liked girls by the time you were sixteen, didn't you?" It came out sounding a little petulant, but it was a question I was sick of hearing. I'd been having wet dreams about men since I was thirteen. I was completely fucking sure I was gay.

He narrowed his eyes at me and nodded, I figured to acknowledge the point. "Okay. Your mom knows?"

"Yes. I told her a few months ago."

He faltered a little at that. I suspected he felt some guilt at not being around more often, but apparently it wasn't enough for him to try harder. My parents' divorce had been messy with a lot of hard feelings on both sides, and I think he was angrier that Mom had won or something than he was about what I'd actually said.

"Well, this doesn't change anything," he said. Then he promptly changed the subject. In retrospect, this is, I think, the best reaction I could have hoped for, but at the time I expected... more. Mom would go on to march in Pride parades with glitter in her hair, but Dad just went about eating his dinner as if nothing I'd said was important. It surprised me how much what he thought of me mattered, and his reaction at that dinner was disappointing.

On the other hand, maybe Dad had the right idea. He would get self-righteous about having a gay son on television later, but at that dinner, he acted as if it was no big deal, and, really, it wasn't. At the time, though, I just looked at my dad and thought: *impossible.*

I WOKE up with Richard Granger on the brain. I'd had a dream in which he'd popped out of closets and corners as if he were a boogeyman, taunting me incoherently. A few times, he'd popped up holding Jonathan—who was tied up and gagged (not in the good way)—and threatened to take him away from me forever. I found upon waking that I was sweating and tangled up in my sheets. I found also that Jonathan was sound asleep beside me.

I watched him for a moment, liking the way his face looked when he was relaxed. His blond eyelashes were so light they were nearly invisible, but they caught the early morning light coming in from the window. There was a dusting of stubble on his chin. His features were otherwise flawless: clean skin, straight nose, high cheekbones. We'd showered before going to bed the night before, and his hair was free of gel and sleep-tousled, and my fingers itched at the memory of running through it. His body was hidden under the covers, but I knew it well by then. I knew the strength that loomed under his skin, I knew how his muscles were formed, I knew how he'd gotten every scratch and scar, and I loved the smattering of hair that went across his chest and lightly over his belly.

I lay there next to him and thought about how I liked his voice, too, and the way he thought about things critically and the way he feigned naïveté sometimes. I thought about the way he'd giggled through the movie we'd watched together the night before, the way he'd noticed things about it that I'd missed, the way he'd made me laugh before he started kissing me until he made me moan.

I looked at him and felt something stir in my chest, and I knew sure as anything that I was falling in love with him.

That felt impossible. I remembered what he'd said to me that first time we'd gone out to dinner: his being gay wasn't an option.

That was what my love for him felt like. It shouldn't have happened, it wasn't an option, but it was there and growing just the same.

I sighed and rolled over, thinking I'd try to go back to sleep, but apparently I'd been ruminating too loudly, because Jonathan stirred. He shifted a little and curled up to me. "Everything all right?" he murmured.

"Swell," I said. "Go back to sleep. I just had a weird dream, is all."

"Mmm." He spooned up behind me, and I could feel his morning erection poking at the small of my back. "Tell me about it."

I most definitely did not want to talk about it, so I said, "I don't really remember."

Jonathan ran a hand over my chest. He kissed the back of my head, then the base of my jaw, near my earlobe. His erection became more persistent than incidental. Mine did too.

He pulled me into his arms and hummed softly. I liked being held by him. His body was warm and languid, and I leaned into him and felt so much comfort there. I decided to push thoughts of Senator Granger and the impossibility of this situation out of my mind and focus instead on the fact that, at least for this moment, I was in bed with Jonathan and he was holding me tightly.

We lay quietly for a long time. I thought maybe he was drifting back to sleep until his hips started to thrust a little against my back. His hands began to roam, too, over my chest mostly, until he started pinching my nipples, and my whole body jerked at the sensation. "Oh, God," I said.

He chuckled softly. "I have you right where I want you."

"Do you now?"

He shifted so that his cock rested between the cheeks of my ass, and he started to thrust his hips with more force. I liked that he was using my body to get off. It was so snug, resting in his arms. I loved the rough texture of his hairy chest against my back. Our bodies seemed to fit together perfectly.

He ran his hands down to my stomach, his palms flat against my abdomen. While thrusting his hips with increasing speed, he moved his hands to the tops of my thighs. My excitement grew as those hands got closer to my cock. I heard him swallow a moan.

"You like that?" I asked him.

"Mmm. I love your body."

"I want to hear how much."

He understood that the way it was intended, and he moaned right in my ear. I shifted my hips back to give him a little more friction. I started to move my hips, too, like my body was moving of its own volition, straining towards his hands. I wanted him to touch me.

But he worked slowly, his hands traveling across my pelvis, grasping at my hipbones, thrusting and rutting behind me towards his own release. Then finally, *finally*, his left hand cradled my balls, and when he squeezed, it was like lightning shooting through my body. His hands were warm and a little rough as he began to grasp and pull at me. He was sighing and moaning behind me, getting closer to his orgasm, and I began to feel like a live wire, all exposed nerve endings, my skin electric.

He wrapped a hand around my cock and started pumping it in an approximation of the rhythm he thrust against my ass.

"I'm gonna come soon," he whispered behind me. "I want you to come too."

"Keep doing that. Faster. Harder."

He complied, pulling and stroking and thrusting. I loved the way his cock slid against my ass, loved that he was getting frenzied and frantic in search of release. I also loved how his long fingers looked wrapped around my cock and how good it felt to have them stroking me. The pace got faster and faster, and everything became like a flurry, him moving behind and in front of me, the scent of him everywhere, and I started to feel overwhelmed.

"Now, Drew. Come for me now."

How could I not? I let the orgasm clobber me, consume me, let all the electrical currents explode, and then I was crying out and clutching my sheets and coming onto his hands. He continued to run his hands over my spent cock after it was over, creating little aftershocks of pleasure that pulsed through my body.

But he wasn't done. He kept on pushing and sliding against me, his rhythm erratic, his breath panting and uneven. Then he bit my shoulder and I felt him coming wet and hot against the small of my back.

We lay tangled for a minute or two. I waited for his breathing to find an even pace again before shifting a little. He pulled at me until I lay on my back, and then he threw a leg over mine. I pulled him close and kissed him. It was a long, tender kiss, with lots of movement, lip biting, and tongue, and I enjoyed every moment of it.

After a little while had gone by, Jonathan propped himself up and said, "Is it cliché to say that no one has ever made me feel as good as you do?"

"Yes, it's a terrible cliché. Doesn't mean I don't like hearing it." In truth, my heart was soaring.

He laughed softly. "Seriously, though. Sex with you blows my mind. You are so fucking hot. Did you know that?"

"You're nice to look at too." I kissed him again. I wasn't very good at taking compliments, and I was worried this could take a maudlin turn.

He smiled. "It's not just sex, though. I feel like, when I'm with you, I've got the whole package. You're hot, but you're also really smart and funny and caring and everything I ever could have dreamed of."

Uncomfortable now, I put a hand over his mouth. "Okay, I'm awesome, I get it."

He grinned. "You are awesome. Don't ever forget it." He lay down and rested his head on my shoulder.

"You're pretty great yourself. I'd list all your good qualities, but I don't want you to get too inflated an ego."

He laughed and it rumbled through his chest. Then he yawned. "God, why am I so sleepy?"

"Because it's early in the morning and you just had really good sex?"

He sighed. "Could be." He snuggled tighter against me and drifted off to sleep.

I liked the weight of his body on mine. I pulled the covers back over us, careful not to move enough to disrupt his sleep. I felt so comfortable and content that, when my eyelids started to get heavy, I let myself drift off with him.

CHAPTER
Fifteen

I WATCHED Jonathan from across the store. He was sliding hangers along racks but didn't seem to be really seeing the clothes. I gave up on him and looked around. I spotted what I'd come into the store to find in the first place: the great shirt I'd seen in the window the week before. And, bonus, now it was on sale.

I walked over to the rack and fished through the shirts until I found one in my size. Then I walked over to Jonathan and held it up to myself. "What do you think?"

He looked at me and squinted at the shirt. "I like the colors."

He was hopeless when it came to fashion. I rolled my eyes. "Okay. What do you think it would look like on me?"

He blinked. Then, much to my dismay, he started to look around the store to see if anyone else was in earshot. Just when I thought we were making progress. It's possible I had bribed him with the prospect of a fancy lunch in order to get him to go shopping with me, but I thought us going out together to do something relatively mundane was a positive step. Watching the shame play out on his face felt like a step back. Besides, the store was empty except for a couple of women gabbing away in front of the accessories display.

It was in that moment that I realized his fear went a lot deeper than being worried he'd get into trouble with his father.

When Jonathan's eyes settled back on me, I said quietly, "Okay, first of all, there's nothing inherently gay about a man telling another man whether or not he'd look good in any given item of clothing. Second of all, we're in Chelsea. Most of this store's clientele is gay. Nothing you say would even raise an eyebrow."

"I think it would look good," he said hesitantly.

I rolled my eyes again. I grabbed his hand and pulled him in the direction of the fitting rooms. "Come with me." I pushed him onto the bench outside the fitting rooms and then went into one of the stalls. "I'll model for you."

I worried briefly that he would bolt, but I could hear him shifting nervously on the bench, the nylon of the jacket he was wearing rustling every time he moved. I pulled off the sweater I'd been wearing and buttoned the new shirt on over my T-shirt. I admired myself in the mirror for a moment, liking the pattern of stripes on the shirt.

There was a knock on the door and a saleswoman said, "Sir, I've got those pants you wanted in a thirty by thirty-six."

I opened the door of the stall just far enough to see the woman. "Such service, thank you," I said. I reached out and she handed me the pants. I closed the door again. I could tell by the clicking of heels on the tiles outside the fitting rooms that the woman was waiting. She tried to start up a conversation with Jonathan, who mostly just grunted in response.

I changed into the pants. They were charcoal gray with subtle pinstripes, and they were very well fitted, maybe even a smidge too tight. I wondered if asking Jonathan for his opinion would be too much teasing, given how tense he seemed over something as innocuous as shopping. On the other hand, it wasn't like I was asking Jonathan to hold my hand on the street. I just wanted some help picking out an outfit for a dinner party I had to go to.

I walked out of the fitting room. Jonathan looked up at me, appraising the outfit. "I like the shirt," he said, almost looking defeated as he said it. Then his gaze settled near my crotch. "The pants look a little tight."

I rotated my body, which gave Jonathan an excellent view of my ass. I looked at the saleswoman. "What's your name, honey?" I asked her.

"Jeanette."

"What do you think, Jeanette? Too tight?"

"Eh, not necessarily. I mean, they are tight, but they look good."

"Would you really want to go out like that?" Jonathan asked. "I mean, I can see your... they don't really leave much to the imagination."

Jonathan looked so uncomfortable that I almost couldn't resist teasing him more. "That's the idea, silly," I told him. I looked at myself in the three-way mirror behind where Jonathan was sitting. I turned around and looked back at my reflection. "I think my ass looks fantastic."

Jonathan laughed despite himself.

"I agree," the saleswoman said.

"Ha, see?" I said to Jonathan. I walked over to Jeanette and leaned over. "You would agree that the goal of any pair of pants is to show off the wearer's ass to its best advantage."

"Sure," she said.

I grinned at Jonathan. "Would you please explain that to my boyfriend?"

Jonathan turned a deep shade of red but didn't protest the label. Then he shook his head. "Your ass looks great in the pants, okay? Your ass always looks great. That doesn't mean everyone has to see it like that."

Well, damn. "Hmm. Well, maybe we could try them on in a size larger," I said to Jeannette.

"Of course," she said with a smile before going off to find another pair of pants.

I looked at Jonathan, sitting on the bench and looking resigned. "I'm sorry."

He shook his head. "No, it's okay."

"I don't know what got into me, I didn't mean to—"

"Drew, it's okay."

Jeannette returned with the pants. I thanked her, then looked at Jonathan. "Hey, was there something you saw that you liked?" I asked. "I saw you eyeing that dark red sweater near the front of the store." I turned to Jeanette. "You know which one I'm talking about?"

"Yup," she said pleasantly. "The V-neck one."

"Uh-huh."

"Yeah, I liked it," Jonathan said. "And, um, I liked those khakis too." He gestured toward a mannequin that was displaying the same sweater in blue and a pair of khakis.

"Geez, you and the khakis. I was thinking that the sweater would look better with those light gray pants over there by the accessories wall. Oh, and you should wear that shirt with the red stripes."

"You don't think it looks a little candy cane?" Jonathan asked.

I laughed, delighted that Jonathan was at least playing along. I thought this was maybe the most couple-y thing we'd ever done together, aside from the sex, of course. He picked out a different shirt, and I sent Jeanette off to grab the clothes. When she was gone, I leaned over and gave him a quick peck on the lips. "See? This is not hard."

"No." He stood on his toes and whispered in my ear, "You'd better change out of those pants. I think everyone here wants to grab your ass."

"And by 'everyone' you mean you?"

Jonathan took a step back and shrugged, which was as close to a *yes* as I thought I would get. I smiled and retreated into the fitting room. When I got the larger pants on, I had to admit that they were a better fit. Still tailored to look good on my body, but much less slutty. I was about to show them to Jonathan when I heard Jeanette come back with the clothes he'd picked out. She installed him in the fitting room next to mine. I heard the tell-tale shuffling of clothes, so I put my own clothes back on and walked out of the fitting room to wait for Jonathan to finish.

He emerged a minute later and said nervously, "What do you think?"

Jonathan wore a shirt and tie to work every day, so seeing him in nice clothes was not a new experience, but there was something about the slightly more stylish, more expensive outfit that transformed him from just a nice-looking man to a force to be reckoned with.

"Wow," Jeanette said.

Jonathan blushed.

"Is that cashmere?" I asked Jeanette.

"Yup. I like it, don't you?"

"Oh, honey. He looks like a million bucks. At least from the front. Turn around, J."

Jonathan dutifully turned around and looked over his shoulder at me. If the goal of every pair of pants was to show off the wearer's ass to its best advantage, this pair achieved its goal and then some. I whistled.

"Shut up," Jonathan said, turning back. He laughed. "You like the outfit?"

"If you don't buy those pants, I'm buying them for you."

Jonathan smiled. He looked at himself in the three-way mirror, fingering the material on the sweater. "I don't usually buy clothes like this," he said. "I mean, this color, it's so... vivid."

"Do you like it?" I asked.

Jonathan considered his reflection. "Yeah," he said at length. "I do."

"Great. Go change so I can buy you lunch."

In the end, Jonathan bought the pants and the shirt for himself. When he hesitated over the sweater, I added it to my pile of clothes and paid for it. He protested, but I wasn't hearing it. When we walked out of the store, each carrying a bag, I expected him to tell me I shouldn't have, but he just said, "Thank you."

"Our relationship may be doomed now," I said. "Buying one's boyfriend a sweater is supposed to be the kiss of death."

"Where did you hear that?"

I waved my hand. "Old wives' tale. How do you feel about sushi for lunch?"

Jonathan sighed happily. "Sure."

I was chagrined to note that Jonathan walked down the street in such a way that he maintained at least a foot of space between us at all times. I knew better than to try to touch him in public, but that distance between us felt like another wall I'd have to pound my way through.

I was busy enough fretting about that space that when Jonathan stopped walking abruptly, I was surprised. I stopped, too, and looked up to see what had caught Jonathan's attention.

There was a couple on the corner of Twenty-First Street: two men, one of them younger, underdressed for the weather in a T-shirt, and the other older and bigger, wearing a studded leather jacket. They were kissing, each of them really absorbed in the kiss, as if no one else in the world existed.

I looked at Jonathan, whose jaw had loosened. When he noticed that I was looking at him, he closed his mouth quickly. "I'm just surprised, is all."

"I hope you know that I would never...."

Jonathan turned to me. "But that's what you want, right? To kiss your boyfriend out in public like that?"

I shrugged. I would have settled for hand-holding, actually. I wasn't that big into public displays. "Not necessarily."

He raised an eyebrow, an expression that said he thought I was lying.

So I conceded. "Yeah, maybe. But I know better. I mean, this stretch of Eighth Avenue is a pretty gay neighborhood, and guys making out on the corner are not really that strange here, but I know better than to think that PDAs like that are kosher everywhere else."

Jonathan nodded. "Okay." Then, quietly, he added, "I'm sorry too."

I smiled at him. "Come on. Sushi awaits."

JONATHAN had other plans that night, so I wound up at a bar with Rey. He was half-watching whatever sporting event was on the television over the bar. We didn't have a lot to say to each other, but often that was okay. We'd perfected the comfortable silence.

Some woman walked up to us. She gasped. "You're Reynolds Blethwyn, right?"

"I think you should deny it," I said to him under my breath.

"I am, yes," Rey said.

"Can I have your autograph?"

Rey grinned. He asked the bartender for a marker. When he asked what she wanted signed, she pulled down her shirt to offer her left breast. Rey winked at her and signed it. The woman squealed and ran off.

"That's disgusting," I said.

"Did you miss the part where I got to sign her boob?"

I rolled my eyes at him. "You are such a fifteen-year-old boy sometimes."

Rey laughed. "Hey, she came to me."

"What happened to not letting all this go to your head?"

He shrugged. "Let me enjoy my fame while it lasts. It could be that tomorrow, *Brooklyn Heights* will get cancelled and then I'll never get another acting gig again."

"That's unlikely."

"I don't know. I wouldn't be the first flash in the pan." He waved down the bartender and ordered another beer. After he took the first sip, he said, "So how's my cousin?"

"Okay. But I thought you didn't want to hear about us."

"I don't. I mean, I don't want to hear about your sex life. But I, you know, was curious, I guess." He shifted his shoulders and took a long sip of his beer.

"Aw, honey. You care!"

"Shut up."

I decided not to goad him too much for his odd show of emotion and instead said, "Things seem to be going fine."

"You don't sound too enthusiastic."

I wasn't sure how to explain it. Telling Rey about the situation with the Senator wasn't necessary and was, I thought, beside the point anyway. "Well, so, we went shopping this afternoon. I have this dinner thing I have to go to next week for the *Forum* staff, and I needed something to wear that would make me look good in photos. So I took Jonathan to that preppy store in Chelsea I like. Getting him to loosen up was like pulling teeth, but then he kind of did and I thought we were good. Then we saw this couple kissing on the street. Gay couple, I should clarify, a beefy leather daddy and a twinky guy in his twenties."

Rey scrunched up his face. "I know there's a point in there somewhere. You always have a point when you go on these little interludes. But I'll be damned if I can work out what it is on my own."

"The *point*," I said, stirring my drink with a straw, "is that Jonathan saw this couple kissing and freaked out a tiny bit. And, you know, I've never been a big proponent of public displays of affection, but he's still so uncomfortable, and I just... it's frustrating, is all."

Rey squinted at me like he was still working out what I was talking about. "That guy you dated a few years ago, the closeted lawyer, what was his name?"

"Kevin."

"Yeah, Kevin. Remember how miserable you were the whole time you dated? How you had to lie that time you were caught out together by one of his coworkers? If I remember correctly, you broke up with him because you knew there was no hope for your relationship if you both continued to lie, because he wasn't ever going to introduce you to his parents or his friends, and you'd always be his piece on the side. Now, I love Jonny, you know that, but do you really think your relationship with him is any different? If anything, it's worse because of Uncle Richard. That Kevin guy was only in the closet because he was a cowardly asshole. Jonny has some good reasons to be afraid."

Rey's speech surprised me. "I can't believe you remember all that."

He shrugged.

"Well, anyway." I paused, still reacting. "Maybe it's not different. But maybe it is. He wants to come out. He's told me as much. And we've had such a great time. I just—"

"I wish you would listen to yourself. You just told me you're frustrated by how uncomfortable he is. It's not just that Jonny is in the closet, it's that he's still not comfortable with being gay. You saw that this afternoon. I mean, forget about Uncle Richard. Isn't *that* the bigger issue?"

I hated Rey a little bit right then. Because he was completely right. "It is, but—"

"Come on. Don't put yourself through this."

I sighed. "What if, Rey? What if he does work it out? What if he figures out how to be comfortable with who he is? What if he figures out what to tell his father? What if he does come out and it becomes a non-issue? What if I dump him before he gets to that point and then I miss out on what could be the best relationship of my life?"

"That's a lot of 'if' to bank on."

"I know, but… I'm not ready to give up on him yet."

"So say you do work things out. It's not as simple as Jonathan accepting that he's gay and then you ride off into the sunset together. You still have to deal with the fact that, because of who his father is, he's going to have attention put on him, especially at first and especially during the campaign. If you're dating him, that means there will be attention on you too. Are you sure you want that?"

I should have known better, but for some reason, it had never occurred to me that I might get pulled into the spotlight also. "Wouldn't be the first time I drew public attention to myself." I wasn't willing to let on that the prospect of that spooked me a little.

Rey stared at me. "What do you see in him, anyway?"

I felt like it was inadvisable to sing Jonathan's physical praises, so I said, "We have fun together, and not just in bed. I think he's interesting. He's funny and flirty when he wants to be and he has this big heart. We can talk about things. He's sort of endearingly naïve."

"Yeah, about that naïve thing. Don't turn him into a project. You do that sometimes."

"What are you talking about?"

"Jonny's a real person, he's not a science experiment. You've made it your mission to get him to come out, but it's complicated."

"I know that. Shit, of course I know that. How can you even say that?"

"I gotta watch out for him too. He's family, after all."

"Of course, but...." I didn't want to have this conversation anymore. Part of me worried Rey was exactly right. Was Jonathan my project? I wanted him to come out; I wanted to help him accept himself. But did I care about that more than I cared about Jonathan? I found it unsettling that the answer to that question didn't come right away. I cared about him, but maybe I'd gotten lost in my mission. "Ugh," I concluded.

Rey chuckled. He slapped my shoulder in an affectionate way, which I think was his way of saying, "We're friends, I have faith in you."

I downed the rest of my drink.

CHAPTER
Sixteen

JONATHAN and I spent a lovely afternoon together, mostly lounging around my apartment and watching rented movies. Then I left Jonathan in my living room while I ran out to buy a few things for dinner. When I got back, I opened the door and sang, "Honey, I have all the ingredients for a marvelous Italian feast!" What I saw first was that Jonathan had a horrified expression on his face, and I was about to ask him what was wrong when I noticed Rey was sitting on my couch. I rolled my eyes and walked past both men into the kitchen, where I deposited my grocery bags on the counter. "Rey," I said when I came back into the living room. "Nice to see you." And I *knew*, I just knew that something really awful was about to unfold.

"Drew, I'm gonna go," Jonathan said, pointing his thumb towards the door.

"But I just got all the stuff to make dinner for us." And all I could think was, *Dammit, Rey, what did you do?* because it was clear he'd said something. I figured he took it upon himself to relate some of what we'd talked about at the bar a few nights before.

"I know," Jonathan said. "I need to leave. I'm sorry. Make dinner for Rey."

He moved towards the door to leave. I followed him into the outside hallway. "What the hell is going on?" I asked when my door slammed shut.

"Rey wants to talk to you about something. He doesn't need me in the way."

"Okay. But that's not the real reason you're leaving. Did Rey say something?"

Jonathan shrugged.

I took his hand. "Jonathan. Come on. Talk to me."

"He just…." Jonathan looked at something on the wall near the stairwell. "He's right, you know. I'm a bad bet."

"What?"

"It's not important." He pulled his hand away. "I can't stay. Rey was right, you deserve more than what I can give you, and something came up, and I really have to go. Please let me go."

He moved toward the staircase, but I grabbed his arm and pulled him back. The look of distress on his face was wrenching. But I couldn't just let him leave, not without a better answer. "At least be honest with me. I deserve that, don't I?"

I could almost see him snap. There was something in the way his eyes changed. He went from watery distress to sharp anger in a flash. "You want honesty?" He pulled his hand away and threw his arms up in the air. "All right, here it is. I'm falling in love with you. I care about you more than anyone I've ever been with. And that's why I have to leave. I will never be the man you want me to be, and if I stay, you'll just end up disappointed and heartbroken, and I don't want that for you. I can't be the man for you. I want you to fall in love with the right man, to live happily ever after and be out and… I don't know, do whatever you want to do. Dance with your boyfriend, hold hands in public, make out on a corner in Chelsea. I can't do any of those things with you. I thought I could, but I just can't. So I have to leave, before we both get in deeper."

My brain processed two parts of that little speech: *I'm falling in love with you* and *I have to leave.* Neither seemed real. A sort of desperate longing lodged itself in my chest. If I let him go, he was leaving for good. And I couldn't let him do that. "But I thought that—"

"I really think it's better if I go. I mean, look at who you are! Everything you do, everything you fight for each day, everything you stand for, it's for gay men to be more accepted. You deserve to be accepted, and you deserve someone who can be totally there for you. You are a wonderful man, Drew, and you deserve everything you want out of life. But I can't give you those things. It's not just my father, it's me too. I'm not ready."

"Don't you deserve everything you want out of life too? I don't know where this is coming from. You're a good person. You deserve love and happiness too."

He shook his head. It was a startling thing, to realize Jonathan *didn't* think he deserved to be accepted and loved. And here I thought we were really building something. It was terrible to realize that he was falling on his sword for my sake. I couldn't let him leave. I needed more time. "I really wish you wouldn't go," I said.

"I know. I don't want to leave."

"Do you think you could—?"

He didn't give me the chance to finish the thought. In that moment, he was gone, disappeared down the stairwell, his footsteps echoing against the old walls of my building.

I turned and walked back into my apartment, not sure if I could take anything more that day. I rubbed my chest where it hurt, and shot Rey a disdainful look as I walked into the kitchen.

"He left?" Rey asked.

I wanted to scream. I wanted to stomp around the apartment and throw things and yell. Rey stood there looking at me like he was a little afraid of what I would do, his hands out in front of him like he was worried I'd attack him.

I looked at the groceries on the counter. Cooking seemed like too much work. "I was going to make chicken parm for me and Jonathan, but now I'm not hungry. Instead, I'm standing in my kitchen with you, who just managed to talk my boyfriend into leaving me. Thanks so much, Rey."

Rey sat at the kitchen table. "You'll wake up tomorrow and realize it was the right thing."

"So you did say something."

"Nothing you haven't probably told him yourself a hundred times. That you deserve someone who's totally committed in a way Jonny is unwilling to be."

"Well, gee, thanks." Some part of my brain decided I should at least put the food away so it wouldn't spoil, but I forgot where everything went. I started opening cabinets and closing them again. I unpacked bags. I put the breadcrumbs in the fridge and the eggs in the cabinet without thinking about it. "What, exactly, did you say?" I stood at the counter, bracing my hands on the edge, unwilling to look at Rey.

He coughed. "I just dropped by, and I found him here. And I said, well…."

I risked glancing back at him. He was staring at the table.

At length, he said, "I wasn't going to say anything. But we got to talking, and he was really tense through the whole conversation. So finally, I stopped him, and I said, 'I know you're gay. I know you've been sleeping with Drew'. So it would be all out in the open, you know?"

How could Jonathan have not known that Rey knew? "Okay. What did he say to that?"

"He sort of freaked out. He said, 'Did Drew tell you? Who else did he tell?' He just went all crazy paranoid on me. I reminded him that he called me before he came over here the first time to hook up with you and also that you're my best friend, so we talked about it but that as far as I knew, I was the only other person on the planet who knew about your relationship."

I sighed. "Well, you and everyone who was at Rooster's that night." I rummaged through the stuff on the counter, but I wasn't sure what I was looking for. "I don't know that anybody we met that night put together than Jonathan was anybody other than some blond guy I'm dating. Among my friends, I mean. Rob and Hal and Darla. They don't know he's Jonathan Granger. I don't think."

"You saw Aaron that night, didn't you? Maybe he guessed correctly and sold you out to the tabloids."

That struck me as out of character for Aaron, and was idle speculation anyway. "Aaron's an asshole, but I really don't think he would do that. And stop distracting me. What else did you tell Jonathan?"

"Just that you're a good guy and you deserve better. I pointed out that he was incredibly uptight around *me*, someone who has been friends with you for years, so I clearly don't have a problem with gay people, and he had a long way to go before he'd be comfortable enough to really make a relationship work with you. That's what I said."

I stared at the vegetables sitting on my kitchen counter for a long moment. The worst part was that I knew deep down that Rey was right, but I was so hurt and angry. "It wasn't your place," I said. "This was my thing to deal with. You should have left it alone. We could have worked something out. He just needed more time. It was not up to you to stick your nose in my life."

"Drew. Come on. You know it's for the best. I did you a favor. He's a bad bet."

Did I know that? I wasn't sure. Probably it was the right thing, for the sake of both our hearts. I tried to see that. Instead, I felt bereft. I turned back to the counter and continued unpacking the grocery bags just so I had something to do with my hands that wasn't strangling Rey. I said, "You know, I'd been thinking lately, maybe being out doesn't matter that much. He'll get to it eventually, and I can wait until then, as long as we get to be together in some way. Time. We just needed more time." I took a deep breath. I was not going to cry, least of all in front of Rey. "Just now? He wasn't just leaving for the evening, he was leaving for good."

"He would have pulled you back into the closet. The whole thing was going to end badly. I really think his leaving is for the best."

"Yeah, that's not really your call. Maybe you did me a favor. Maybe I just let the man I'm supposed to spend the rest of my life with walk away. I guess time will tell. But I don't want to talk about it anymore."

"Fine."

I slammed a head of lettuce on the counter and turned around. He sat there, leaning into the chair, his legs crossed, staring unfocused at something in the corner. I screamed something incoherent while I came up with something to say to him that really conveyed how I was feeling, and the best I came up with was, "Fuck you."

"Now hold on a minute," Rey said, uncrossing his legs and sitting up straight.

"Fuck you, Rey. What the hell gives you the right to come in here and mess with my life? Why would you do that?"

He looked back at me, his eyes wide. He moved his lower jaw, and then he said, "I… I want things to work out for you. I don't know."

I closed my eyes for a long time, trying to get a grip. I was mad, but I knew Rey's heart was in the right place. I leaned against the counter. "Why are you here, Rey? There better be a damned good reason."

"You're not really upset with me."

"I am, actually."

"Look, I'm sorry. Okay? I'm sorry. And I know how it is. Everyone I date lately only wants me for my fame."

"Oh, geez. You have such problems."

Rey huffed. "So, fine. I've got women who want me to autograph their breasts but can't find anyone who wants to go out with me on a second date. You've got closeted boyfriends. Shit never works out the way it's supposed to."

I rubbed my eyes. I was so tired. "Hell, you and me, we'll probably end up sitting on a porch at the end of time, just two lonely old men."

"Sounds like fun." He let out a breath. "I actually came over to ask you to run some lines with me. Like we did in old times? I got the script for that new movie I'm doing."

That seemed to diffuse the situation. When Rey was first starting to get roles, I used to run lines with him all the time. I was not a very good actor, but he swore he just needed someone to speak the other part. We hadn't done it in a while, though. I appreciated that he was trying to reach out to me, which made it hard for me to stay mad at him.

There was still food on the counter and I noticed that I was suddenly hungry. "Sure, I'll run lines. Let's do dinner first though, huh? Nothing like getting your heart broken to give you an appetite."

Although my first instinct had been to push Rey out the window, I wasn't able to face being alone just yet, so I let him stick around and try to make amends. When cooking proved impossible for me, he helped me set my kitchen to rights and ordered us a pizza. We talked about stupid shit while we ate, mostly gossip about our mutual friends and ridiculous things we'd seen on TV. He surprised me by mentioning something he'd read in my column the week before; that impressed me because I didn't think he read it anymore. He steered clear of mentioning family or politics, which was just as well, because I felt myself calming down.

We got to the line reading a little while later. Rey squirmed on the couch while I read the script. I was having a hard time concentrating. In part, this was because he was staring at me, which I found unnerving, but also my mind was still on Jonathan.

Finally, I finished and said, "Wow, this is a pretty intense scene."

"You can see why I wanted to do the movie."

"Yeah. I can't get over that you get offered movies like this. Or that I knew you when you were just hoping to get cast in Montrose High's production of *The Odd Couple*."

"We've come a long way since then, haven't we?"

We had. Which was why I hadn't kicked Rey out of my apartment; I was still plenty angry that he'd taken it upon himself to intervene in my love life, but I understood why he'd done it.

After a long silence, he said, "I'm sorry for earlier. Well, I'm not sorry for yelling at Jonny, but I am sorry you're so upset."

I shrugged. "It's all right."

"It's not all right." He grunted. "I should have let you deal with it. I acted out of turn. I shouldn't have meddled. You're allowed to be pissed at me."

We sat there silently for a long moment. I couldn't think of a thing to say.

Very quietly, Rey said, "Jonny's family, but I did it for you."

"What?"

Rey sat on the end of the couch. His gaze shifted towards the television. "I care about what happens to him, I do, but I was thinking of you when I opened my mouth to talk to him. I did it for you. I hate seeing you hurt."

"Oh."

I handed the script back to him. He took it and dropped it next to his bag on the floor. He reached over and patted my shoulder. He smiled sadly. Then he pulled me into his arms for a hug.

Which was pretty fucking weird. Rey and I did not hug.

But I sank into his arms and let him hold me and I thought about all the times when we'd been kids that I'd wanted a moment like this to happen. How I'd sit next to him in the movies or in school and wish that he'd notice me in the way I noticed him. Obviously, I'd moved past that before we hit adulthood, but his hugging me now seemed romantic in a way.

I wasn't thinking clearly, is my point. Rey's shoulder was warm where my cheek lay against it, and he smelled amazing—his aftershave had kind of a pine-y zip to it—so I pulled away slightly to look at him. Our eyes met. Then I kissed him.

He barely reacted at first. Then his lips moved against mine, probably by instinct. There was no heat in it, though, no particular spark. The kiss felt chaste and a little incestuous. Finally, my brain registered that I was kissing Rey, and I pulled away abruptly. Rey sputtered in surprise.

"Hmm," I said.

Rey wiped at his mouth. His eyebrows moved from raised shock to lowered anger. "What the hell was that?"

"It was a thing to do."

"I'm not gay."

"I know."

Rey crossed his arms over his chest, then sat back on the couch. "Maybe I should leave."

God. Could I have fucked up this day any more? "I'm sorry. I shouldn't have done that. I'm in a pissy mood, I guess. I was feeling taken advantage of."

"So you *kissed* me?" His voice went a little shrill.

"I know. It was a shitty thing to do."

Rey frowned. "I didn't mean to take advantage of you. I just thought…."

"I know what you thought. I get it." I stood up. "Maybe you *should* go. Leave me to wallow melodramatically in my own pathos, worrying about how I will never find love." I mock swooned, tilting my head back and placing the back of my hand on my forehead.

"You're a real Olivier, you know that?"

If he was making jokes, I figured the damage to our friendship caused by the kiss was minimal. "Get out of here, Rey. Go practice reading lines or whatever it is you do with your off time. I promise not to kill myself while you're gone."

Rey stood and gathered his things. "Jonny's a good guy at heart, but I just don't think—"

"Stop apologizing. I get it."

He shoved all of his things in his bag, then picked it up and turned to me. "Still, I—"

"Let's not talk it to death."

Rey nodded. "I'm going to go home. Uh. Thanks. For dinner and all that. I'll see you around, Drew." Then he left.

CHAPTER
Seventeen

IN THE long, storied history of my friendship with Rey, there was one moment that almost broke us. We both went to NYU, so we decided to room together freshman year. This was not a wise decision on a number of levels, not the least of which was that Rey was clearly not comfortable with the situation: he wouldn't change clothes in the room if I was around, he'd make himself scarce if I had boys over, he made me take down the poster of my favorite actor shirtless, and so on. I'd come out to him when we were juniors in high school, and he knew about my first boyfriend, Pete, but my sexuality was something we just did not talk about ever. And because I was a petulant teenager, I wanted to throw it in his face.

Things came to a head, so to speak, one afternoon. I was kind of seeing this guy Jake. He was a big burly redhead, which is not usually my type, but something about his hyper-masculine affect really got to me. He was overcompensating, of course; I was not to tell a soul he let me fuck him. But let me fuck him he did, and that was exactly what I was doing in my dorm room that afternoon when Rey came charging in.

As soon as I heard the key in the lock, I pulled a sheet over me and Jake, but I was still inside him when Rey came into the room. To say that it was awkward would be an understatement. I lost my hard-on and had to find a way to extract myself from Jake without Rey catching on to what was really happening.

Rey, naturally, was horrified. He yelled and screamed a lot and then stormed right back out of the room. Jake was mortified that he'd gotten caught, so he pushed me off him, pulled his clothes on, and stormed out as well. I never did see Jake again after that.

Rey vanished for a couple of days. I think he slept at his girlfriend's place. But he found me in the dining hall at lunch one afternoon. He sat across from me and said, "I don't think we should room together next year."

I didn't need to ask him why. I just nodded. I knew it was probably for the best. I'd been thinking it might be better to room with someone like my friend Mike—the one who would go on to do drag. We were totally platonic, but I thought having a gay roommate would make things easier. He'd be less afraid of me, for one thing.

Then Rey said, "Also, I don't want you bringing guys to the room anymore."

"What? But you bring your girlfriend over all the time!"

"That's different."

"How is it different?"

"She's a girl."

I couldn't believe Rey was the one I was having this argument with. I said that I would not apologize for who I was, that he was being hypocritical and unfair, and then I told him to go fuck himself before I picked up my tray and stomped out of the dining hall.

It felt like a breakup. I honestly thought we would not be friends anymore after that. Obviously that wasn't the case, but I always had this nagging doubt in my mind that Rey was horrified and embarrassed by me. So despite what he'd said, after he left my apartment, I couldn't help but wonder if he didn't want me to be with Jonathan because he didn't want me spreading the gay to his cousin, or whatever delusional thing he might be thinking. And the thing was that I could find a way to cope with losing Jonathan. I cared about him a great deal—shit, I was in love with him—and his leaving felt awful, but I'd manage. The thought of Rey losing faith in me or freaking out again like he had when we were in college was something I didn't want to face. I could not lose Rey. He was my best friend. He was my brother.

IT WAS a tearjerker-movie-and-pints-of-ice-cream kind of night. I had draped myself along the foot of Allie's bed while Allie sat cross-legged behind me, the television blaring. She lived in a tiny studio in which the bed took up most of the space, but she had a great TV. (She had her priorities sorted out.) We were most of the way through *Beaches*, to which I wasn't really paying attention, when she started talking.

I'd told her about Jonathan one night. A few nights after he broke up with me, while I was still a little mad at Rey (and, okay, still embarrassed that I'd kissed him), I went to Allie because I needed someone to talk to. I'd sat on her bed and told her the whole story. I'm sure parts of it were incoherent, and I went through half a box of tissues, but she sat across from me and listened patiently.

When it was done, she took her turn to talk. She was upset that I'd kept something like that from her, but claimed to understand. She gave me a hug and told me she hoped everything would work out for me. It wasn't much comfort, but talking about it was cathartic, and it was nice to spend time with a friend.

But I still didn't really feel much better. Hence all the ice cream. We'd had a lot of nights with sad movies and junk food in college, sort of a tradition that emerged anytime one of us got dumped or flunked an exam or whatever, so I'd called Allie a week after I'd told her about Jonathan and declared an ice cream emergency.

There's that scene in the movie when Bette Midler and Barbara Hershey get all sentimental, right before Barbara Hershey's character dies, and it made me cry like a baby every damn time I see it, but Allie distracted me by saying, "You going to the *Brooklyn Heights* wrap party?"

"Yeah." The party was still a few weeks away, but I'd already decided. I felt sort of obligated. Rey had sent me a formal invitation, but the last few times we'd spoken on the phone, things had been stilted. I think he was more wigged out by the kiss than he was letting on. So now that things with Rey were weird, I felt like I had to make it up to him somehow.

Allie nodded. "What if Jonathan's there?"

"Why would he be there?"

She ate a substantial spoonful of ice cream. "He's Rey's cousin."

"It doesn't matter. It's over."

Allie scooped some ice cream out of her pint container and held it out for me. I ate it. She said, "You know, it doesn't have to be this way. It's possible you might still work things out."

I waved my hand. "I don't think so. Everything's fucked."

"Jonathan might see the light."

I very much doubted that. "I think it's better if I stay away." I reached for the cookies 'n cream. "And while we're recounting my failures, I did something stupid last week."

"Yeah?"

"I didn't tell you, but Rey and I kind of had a moment. When he was apologizing for sticking his nose in the Jonathan drama, he hugged me, which was really weird. So I got it into my head that I should kiss him. He was so shocked and disgusted by it that he spit and wiped his mouth. The worst part is that I don't even know what came over me, except that I apparently have some kind of death wish."

"Really? Did you really kiss him?"

"Yup, I really did. The real irony here is that I don't really feel that way about Rey anymore. I haven't in a long time, many years. It's more like nostalgia. I spent so many of my formative years wanting him, and then we were hugging and I took the opportunity more out of habit, if you get what I'm saying, but he's not what I want anymore."

"What do you want?" Allie asked.

I sighed and flopped down on my back on the bed. "Jonathan. I want Jonathan."

"But you said him leaving you was for the best. That it's over."

"I did say that. It probably is. And I'm doomed to spend the rest of my life miserable and alone."

"You are such a drama queen."

"Just indulge me for now, all right? I'll get it all out of my system." I ate a big gulp of ice cream. "I deserve to be with someone who is not ashamed of who he is, who is not ashamed of us. I deserve to be with someone who doesn't have to hide. I know that. But it doesn't mean I don't miss him."

"So you're giving up?"

"What else is there to do? Even if I were willing to compromise on the being out thing, which I know that I shouldn't, he's the one who left me, remember?"

Allie just shook her head. "What else indeed?"

"I know I'm being dramatic. But I will not be dragged back into the closet." I waved my spoon in the air with no small amount of flourish.

"Like anyone could drag you back."

As I perused the menu at a café in Manhattan a few days later, I said, "You know, the fare here leaves something to be desired."

"You picked this place," Rey pointed out.

I'd invited Rey to brunch as a peace offering. It had seemed like a good idea to try a new venue, so I had solicited recommendations from Hal and settled on a little café near Central Park. The offerings, however, were a little paltry, mostly small portions of healthy foods. "You know what I really want?" I asked. "Pancakes. And sausage. Covered in chocolate."

Rey laughed. "That does sound good."

"I'd ruin my girlish figure, though." I tugged on the waistband of my jeans. "I think I've put on a little weight as it is. I gotta lay off the Ben & Jerry's. These pants are a little snug. Did you notice? Is my ass getting bigger?"

"I don't spend much time looking at your ass, as a rule."

"Hmm. Some friend you are. I want you to know that if I ever notice your ass has grown, I will tell you."

"I appreciate that."

A very cute waiter (what? I'm human) came by to take our orders. After he was gone, Rey asked, "How are you doing?"

I knew he was asking specifically how I was coping with my break up with Jonathan. I opened my mouth to say I was fine, but the truth was that I was a mess. Still. "I miss him. A lot."

"Yeah, I know."

"Have you seen him?"

Rey hesitated, which I took as a yes. He said, "We went out last week. Just to a bar near my place." He shook his head. "And, uh, we had dinner with Uncle Richard when he was in town."

"How nice for you."

"Yeah, well. Dad came, too, and it turned into this whole tortured awkward thing." He furrowed his brow. "Despite the perfectly unpleasant time had by all, Richard keeps calling me."

"To talk about Jonathan or the campaign?"

"Mostly the campaign. He wants my endorsement, which I expected. Thinks being seen in public with me will get him the youth vote. I told him I didn't feel comfortable getting involved in politics. Then I told him that having a Hollywood type endorsing him would probably piss off his base, but he thought my relative fame would outweigh that. What I should have done was tell him to shove it, because he's not letting up on this idea that a few words from me will win him the election. I'm not sure what to do there."

"I don't know what you should do, either. That's a tough situation. Maybe you should appeal to his sense of image. Tell him that, for the sake of your career, you don't want to be affiliated with any particular political party. You're worried about your public image. He should understand that."

"Yeah." Rey looked down. "He also asked me to check up on Jonny, make sure he wasn't further disgracing the family name."

I rolled my eyes, but deep down, that hurt. "Did you assure him this was not the case?"

The food arrived before Rey could answer. He waited until the waiter was gone before speaking again. "I'm sorry."

I felt like I'd been punched in the gut. I put my fork aside, my appetite suddenly gone. I stared at my omelet for a few moments. Very quietly, I said, "What I felt when Aaron left, that was nothing." I picked up my fork again and poked at my food. "Not to be melodramatic. I mean, I'll get through this. Right as rain in a few months. Right?"

"Of course."

"How is he?"

"I think in about the same place you are."

I looked up.

Rey said, "We deal with shit like this in different ways. You tend to become a hermit. I start shouting at people. He… drinks a lot."

That sounded about right.

"Look," Rey said. "I feel sort of responsible for what happened."

"Don't."

"No, I do. I…." He shook his head. He was silent for a long time, pushing fruit around on his plate. He whispered, "I hate seeing you like this."

I felt tears spring to my eyes. I blinked them away, but I was touched by the emotion in his voice. "Rey."

"We've known each other a long time," he said.

"You don't have to do this." I rubbed my forehead. "You always do this mopey confessional 'I love you, man' thing when things go wrong with us, and you don't have to. I know. I appreciate that you're my friend and you're trying to help me through this. But it wasn't your fault, what happened with Jonathan. I'm coming to realize that you just sped up the inevitable. And then I fucked it up by kissing you, which I shouldn't have done, and I was way more out of line, so I should be apologizing. I *am* sorry, genuinely so. I hope you know that."

"I do know that. And that wasn't what I was going to say." Rey tapped the table in front of me. I looked up from my omelet. He took a deep breath. "This is not easy for me to tell you."

"What?" I asked, not having the first clue what might come out of Rey's mouth. I felt nervous, suddenly.

"We've known each other a long time. Mrs. Pearl's class, right?"

"Yes, of course. I don't see what this has to do with anything. Yes, we've been friends for a hell of a lot of years."

"I've made some mistakes in my life, especially recently," Rey said. "Probably I will continue to make them, as will you. I try to look at what's happened and learn from it. And do you want to know what I figured out this time?"

"I'll bite."

Rey sat there for a moment, gathering his thoughts. "It occurred to me after I left your apartment last week that I'd really fucked up. I've always stayed out of your love life, but this time, I got involved. And I thought, *fuck.* What if you chose Jonny instead of me?" He swallowed, suddenly becoming choked up. I was surprised; I couldn't think of a time when I'd ever seen Rey this emotional. He fought not to show it too. "Jonny's my cousin, yeah, but you're the closest thing I ever had to a brother, to a real family, and I don't know what I would do without you."

The words meant a lot, coming from Rey. I didn't know how to respond. Despite my own years spent pining for Rey, I knew that somewhere along the line, that tension between us had eased and we'd settled into a friendship that was good and vital for both of us. "I'm not going anywhere," I said softly. "I don't plan to. Come on, Rey. You know you're the best friend I ever had."

A pained look came over Rey's face. Then he nodded slowly. "Yeah." We both went about eating silently for a while. I found that my appetite had returned somewhat. I supposed the silver lining was that Jonathan and men like him had come and gone and would probably continue to come and go in the future, but Rey was the constant. He'd date women who were all wrong, I'd endure bad breakups, and we'd help each other through it same as always. I took some comfort in that.

Rey was the one who broke the silence. Almost inaudibly, he said, "Thank you."

"Yeah. So tell me about the *Brooklyn Heights* finale. I need the inside scoop, man. What happens in the last few episodes?"

He smirked, and apparently things were back to normal. He talked about the show with the same "I can't believe this is my life" tone he usually used. We laughed about how absurd everything was. I felt like I had my best friend back.

CHAPTER
Eighteen

IN THE weeks after Jonathan left me, the Granger for President campaign began to kick up into high gear. Granger flew around the country to give speeches and kiss babies while he and the four other Republican candidates competed for media attention. Primary season was a few months away, and at that point, it really was anyone's race. The punditry generally seemed stumped about who would walk away with the nomination. Because, yeah, Granger was an arch-conservative these days, but he was savvy in public appearances, and he was handsome and charming, too, and apparently TV audiences ate that up.

My editor Wade, of course, wanted me to write about it. He was pushing me to write columns on the election generally and my alleged nemesis Granger particularly. Under other circumstances, I might have been all over that, but I just couldn't bring myself to write about Granger anymore. I knew too much about him, for one thing; he'd become a real person instead of a character in my head, which made it harder to write harsh things. Also, I was worried it would get back to Jonathan and he'd be hurt or angry or think I was being petty.

Instead, I wrote about the gay character on a new teen soap. I turned in a column on the latest pop singer to come out on a magazine cover. Pop culture was really more my milieu, anyway. I told Wade I wasn't sure I should be writing about politics anymore.

Then a civil unions bill came up for a vote in one of the Midwestern states, and it seemed everyone in gay media was all over it. My buddy Libby Madden cajoled me into doing a few segments on her cable show, and I agreed on the condition we not talk about Granger or the primary race. Luckily, her producers didn't ask why.

I perhaps got a little maudlin. Let that be a lesson to you about discussing marriage when you're nursing a broken heart. I was cynical on the air, telling the viewing audience that I thought the bill was a step in the right direction, but that gay activists tended to put all their eggs in one basket whenever bills like this were introduced, assuming that another state legalizing civil unions or even full-on marriage equality would be the domino that caused all of the other states to pass similar bills, which I knew wouldn't be the case. Libby pointed out that the recent news of New York legalizing same-sex marriage could very well go a long way toward affecting the outcome of votes in other states. I told her it was small consolation that, if I should ever fall in love, I could at least get married in my adopted state (though still not in my home state of New Jersey, where my mother still lived). My voice cracked when I said "fall in love," but luckily, nobody noticed. Libby's assistant stood off camera and made faces at me through most of my segment, her way of telling me I was being too negative. I was there to be funny, not to rain on their parade. But I was right; ultimately, the bill failed.

When Aaron had dumped me, I'd moped around and been sad and missed him for weeks, but that all felt like a trifle compared to what I felt in Jonathan's absence. I didn't have to avoid him because there was no way he'd show up at any of my usual haunts, and yet I couldn't escape him. It was bad enough that his father was on TV at least once a day. On top of that, memories would sneak up on me when I didn't expect them to. I'd lie in bed at night and think about him and what it felt like to have him lying next to me. I'd be sitting on my couch and have some flash of memory of us laughing or talking or cuddling in front of a movie. One afternoon, I walked by the restaurant at which we'd had our first date and nearly broke down; I had to duck into a coffee shop to drown my sorrows in a sugary latte.

Rey wasn't around much in those weeks, either. He was busy alternately filming his new movie and doing press for the one he'd shot in Prague, and that was in addition to filming the last few episodes of that season of *Brooklyn Heights*. So he was out of town a lot, or if he was in town, he was working. I was glad that things with us were settled and back to normal before he got sucked into all that.

He'd call every couple of days to make sure I was all right. I couldn't lie to him, so I told him the truth: I was still upset, but I was trying to keep my mind off of it by keeping busy.

One night he called and said, "Hey, I managed to catch you on Libby's show last night."

"Yeah?" Learning her lesson about making me talk about politics, Libby had gotten me to come on the show to talk about a former Miss North Carolina who, it turned out, was a lesbian. She had a new memoir coming out and was doing this insane media blitz, hitting all the talk shows to opine about how hard it was to be a gay beauty queen. I always felt like such a dork when I went on television, but preparing for the show was a nice distraction, and besides, strange moments in pop culture were things I was happy to talk about.

"Don't take this the wrong way," Rey said, "but you looked good."

I laughed. I knew exactly what he meant. "I've been sleeping a lot lately, so that's probably part of that." I'd been going to the gym too. I'd never been big on working out, but I found I was able to sleep better if I put myself through the rigors of exercise in the evening. Plus, there was a really hot guy at my gym who was prone to walking around without a shirt when he got good and sweaty. Talk about a nice distraction.

"How are things?" Rey asked.

"Eh, about the same as the last time I talked to you. What about you?"

"I have to fly to London on Thursday."

"Your life is so hard, Rey. How do you stand it?"

He sighed. "It's not really a pleasure trip. I'm flying out Thursday morning, I'll spend the day cooped up in a hotel room doing interviews, and I'll go to the premiere at night. I'm staying overnight, but I have an early flight back to New York Friday so that I can make it in time to shoot my last scene for *Brooklyn Heights*. Then the wrap party's on Sunday."

"I've always wanted to go to London."

"So go. Doesn't that trashy newspaper pay you? Surely you can afford it."

Oh, Rey. If he had one personality flaw, it was that he had the strange naïveté of someone who had always had money. It never occurred to him that other people didn't. "Maybe next summer," I said, not wanting to start an argument. "Isn't London cold and dreary at this time of year?"

"Isn't it always?"

There was a pause in which I pondered what else to say. It popped into my head and then out of my mouth faster than I could stop it. "I read an article yesterday on some gossip blog saying that you're Senator Granger's nephew."

"Yeah," he said, sounding weary. "In some ways, I guess it's good that the information is out there. If he's gonna use me anyway, it might as well be as a fun trivia fact. I hope it's enough to get him off my back."

"No one would think less of you if you stumped for your uncle. It's how the game is played."

There was a long pause, but I could hear Rey breathing into the phone, so I knew he was still there. Eventually, he said, "I can't. How can I? How can I publicly endorse a man who thinks my best friend shouldn't have rights?"

"Rey, it's okay."

"And after everything that happened with Jonny? He's dating a woman now, you know."

I hadn't known, actually. That news stabbed me like a knife through the heart. I had been pacing around my living room before that, but when Rey dropped that bomb, I had to sit down. I half-fell onto my couch. "He's what?"

"That teacher at school he went out with right before he hooked up with you. They're sort of seeing each other, according to the family grapevine. I asked Jonny about it and I get the impression they haven't, uh, sealed the deal yet, but they've gone on a few dates."

My heart broke all over again, and not just for my own sake. I worried for Jonathan. I saw this future play out for him in which he spent the rest of his life trapped in a marriage to a woman he couldn't love, alone and compliant and miserable. I felt oddly devastated for him; even if he wasn't with me, I wanted him to be happy, but dating a woman was not going to work out for him.

Rey said quietly, "I understand now why that won't work out. The whole situation sucks. And Uncle Richard is responsible for creating it in large part. I mean, Jonny's acting on his own, obviously, but how can you grow up gay in a house like theirs and not hate yourself? I can't endorse Richard, I just can't."

I was close to losing it then. It had been almost a month since Jonathan had left, and the pain was still raw. I wondered if I'd ever get over it. "I love him," I said.

Rey gasped. After a moment, he said with a little mirth, "Uncle Richard?"

"Ha, ha, asshole. No, your delusional cousin. I'm still stupidly head-over-heels in love with the man who walked out of my life weeks ago."

I had never told Rey this. He took a moment to ponder it. Finally, he said, "I wish I didn't have to be on set tomorrow. I'd take you out and make you drink gin and tonics until you can't even remember Jonny's name."

It was Rey's way of being there for me. I appreciated the sentiment. "It's fine, fancy movie star. I'll forgive you if you get me into the New York premiere of your movie. Tickets are apparently a hot item."

"Not a problem. You are coming to the wrap party, right?"

My turn to sigh. He *had* invited Jonathan, he'd already told me that, but he didn't think his cousin would put in an appearance. Still, it seemed to me that there was a risk he would.

"Would it help if I told you that all of my more attractive male costars will be at the party? I know you have a thing for Rene." Rene was a French actor who played a swarthy businessman on the show.

"Yeah, yeah, I'll be there."

"Good. These parties aren't the same without you."

I felt suddenly exhausted. "Well, on that note."

"Yeah, I gotta go too. Take care of yourself, Drew."

"I will. Try to enjoy yourself in London."

"I will."

After Rey was off the phone, I lay down on my couch and stared at the ceiling for a while. I decided to be optimistic. There was a big party to attend, and columns to write, and life would carry on. I'd meet other men and probably get my heart broken again a time or two. I wished Jonathan the best but knew it was out of my hands. I got up, deciding I'd start my new optimistic phase by going to visit my shirtless, well-muscled friend at the gym. I figured, if anything, a half hour on a treadmill would tire me out enough that I'd sleep through the night and put off worrying about everything until the next day.

CHAPTER
Nineteen

WHEN I got to the *Brooklyn Heights* wrap party, I was surprised to see a cavalcade of paparazzi outside. I guessed this was de rigueur for these kinds of events, but somehow I hadn't anticipated it.

Rey had encouraged me to find a date, but I hadn't had the energy. I walked in alone. The paparazzi at the door seemed to think I was important, but I convinced them I was a nobody, just some friend of the crew. I gave my name to the bouncer and he let me in.

The party was buzzing; there were easily over one hundred people crammed into the restaurant. The place had a dark pink interior with thick curtains covering all the windows, and the tables had been removed, so everyone was standing. There was music and dancing and a small fleet of cocktail waitresses offering canapés and hors d'oeuvres. I spotted Rey on the other side of the room, impossibly far away, deep in conversation with one of his costars.

I walked through the crowd and snagged some sort of chicken thing on a toothpick before a waitress stopped and asked if I wanted a drink. I ordered and opted to stay put, lest the waitress not be able to find me again.

"Excuse me," a male voice said over my shoulder. I turned around to see a guy with a press pass hanging around his neck. He was trailed by a photographer with a huge camera in his hands. The reporter had a digital recorder. "You're Andrew Walsh, right? Of the *Forum*?"

"Uh. Yeah, that's me." I wondered why this guy would care.

"I recognized you from Libby Madden's show. Are you here in an official capacity? Are you covering the party?"

"No. I'm an invited guest. Unlike you, I suspect."

The reporter nodded as if he hadn't heard the last part. "I wonder why a man who writes about gay issues would be at a party like this."

I raised an eyebrow at the reporter. "It's a little known fact that some gay men have interests outside of being gay." I shook my head. "I don't know why you care about me. I'm a friend of the show, okay? You can put that in your article. I'm not here to write a column, I'm just here to have a good time. All right? Go away."

I started to move, but the reporter was persistent. "You *are* gay, right?"

"What do you think?"

"There are rumors linking you romantically to Reynolds Blethwyn. Care to comment?"

"No. Reynolds and I are old friends. That's all."

"What about the rumor that you're the man Senator Granger's son Jonathan was seen with at a gay club in October?"

I balked. I was so surprised that my negative reaction was probably convincing. "No comment."

I mean, Rey, okay. We went out together all the time, and enough people in the city knew who I was that it didn't surprise me that rumor had us dating, especially after that spate of gay rumors a few months before. But it was news to me that anyone had identified me as the mystery man who was caught kissing Jonathan at Rooster's. I felt panic rising but managed to tamp it down. It didn't really matter much anymore, I figured. Jonathan was no longer a part of my life.

The waitress returned with my drink. I had ordered a glass of red wine but was thinking now that I wanted something I could drink faster. I considered ordering a gin and tonic, but I thanked her and took a big gulp of wine instead. It burned in my throat all the same. I turned to the reporter. "Can't you go pester someone else who will actually tell you something interesting? Isn't there an extra or somebody here who wants to be famous that you can bug? I have no comment on anything."

"But you know both Reynolds Blethwyn and Jonathan Granger personally."

I hesitated but didn't want to lie. He was going to find out anyway. "Yes."

"Can you confirm that Jonathan Granger is gay?"

"Nope."

"No he's not gay or no you won't confirm it? I have it on good authority that he was in that club kissing a man. Kissing you."

"I have no comment. I told you to go away."

"Because that would be quite a story, don't you think? The Senator's son being gay? You in particular could get a lot of mileage out of a story like that. Or are you having an affair after all? I mean, that's juicy, a gay activist and vocal critique of Senator Granger having a big gay affair with his son?"

I drank another big gulp of wine. "There's no affair. I'm done talking," I said.

I beat a hasty retreat and beelined for Rey, who had ended his conversation and was casually wandering through the party. I grabbed his wrist and pulled him close to me. "Who let the press in here?" I hissed.

He pulled his wrist away. "Nice to see you too."

I tried to relax, but as the minutes ticked by I grew increasingly angry. I took a deep breath. "Sorry. I just got accosted by a reporter, and it put me in a bad mood. Congratulations on wrapping the season and all that."

"Thanks." He grinned. "Did you hear the news? We just got picked up for another season!"

"Oh. Congrats!" I felt a little better, basking in his glow a bit. I scanned the room. Then I saw.... "Holy crap."

"What?"

"Jonathan's here."

"Yeah. I mean, you knew I invited him. I felt bad about—"

I didn't give him a chance to finish. I wasn't that interested in apologies. "Should I go talk to him? Maybe I shouldn't. The reporter over there is trying to link us romantically. He knows about Rooster's. If Jonathan and I are seen together, the rumors will probably just get worse."

Rey held up his hands. "It's your call, Drew. I won't get involved anymore."

Sure, *now* he decided to butt out. "Gee," I said. I spent a good long moment staring and trying to figure out what to do. Jonathan was talking to a dark-haired woman and didn't seem to notice me.

Rey was speaking, but I didn't hear him until he said, "Actually, I think what I should really do is have an affair with a space alien."

"What?"

Rey sighed. He grabbed my arm. "Please pay attention. You should know, Jonny brought a date. A lady date."

Of course he did. I turned and looked at Rey. "Well, that figures."

"It's the teacher he's been seeing."

"Ah." Shit. "So his beard."

Rey shrugged. I closed my eyes for a long time, then opened them again, hoping Jonathan would be gone. I was almost disappointed to find myself still at the party. I didn't think I could get through a whole night with Jonathan so close and *not* speak to him.

When I turned away to look at Rey, he was looking at me with his eyes narrowed.

"What?"

He scratched his nose. "You're not going to give me a 'How could you do this to me?' speech? You're not mad I invited him?"

"He's your cousin."

"He's your ex-boyfriend."

It popped into my head that I'd recently read a book in which the author overused the word *ineffable*. It seemed to fit here. This situation was ineffable. "I'm not mad at you. Aren't we past this?"

"Okay, good. How are you going to handle the situation here?"

I decided I should probably get it out of the way. "I think I'm going to go get my heart trampled on now."

Rey patted me on the back. "Go get 'em, tiger."

I turned to him and raised an eyebrow. "Really? 'Go get 'em, tiger'?"

Rey laughed. "I don't know. Break a leg? Good luck? Come find me after you talk to him."

"Yeah, I will."

I approached slowly. I decided that the woman hanging on Jonathan was pretty enough, if a little plain. I will admit that I had a "What does he see in her?" moment, but of course, I knew: she didn't have a penis. I also knew she wasn't what he wanted. But there she was, hanging on his arm. Her eyes were wide, taking in all the celebrities mingling at the party.

I interrupted their conversation. "Jonathan."

He about jumped out of his skin. He turned towards me, his eyes wide with shock. Then he looked down. He didn't say anything.

"Can I talk to you for a moment?" I asked.

The woman looked me over. "Andrew Walsh! It's nice to meet you. I'm Lisa."

Out of habit, I extended my hand for her to shake. "Nice to meet you. Uh, call me Drew." It was like a reflex, speaking to her, though I really didn't want to. In the back of my mind, I kind of thought of her as the enemy. She hadn't even done anything, poor thing.

"This is so great." She smiled. Her gaze passed between us. "I read the article, of course. Have you guys been hanging out since it was published?"

Actually, it had been a month since we'd done anything. Jonathan said, "In a manner of speaking." He seemed to be scanning her face, probably to see if she'd cottoned on to the nature of our relationship.

But she was delightfully oblivious. "Are you here to do a story about the show?" she asked me.

"No, but you're not the first person to ask. I'm just here as an invited guest. I've been friends with Reynolds Blethwyn for years."

"Oh, that's funny! How do you know Reynolds?" She giggled as she said the name, as if she were tickled to be on a first-name basis with him.

"We went to school together," I said.

"Really? You're friends with someone that famous, but you've never mentioned him in your column?"

Was she a regular reader? I guess that was how she knew who I was right away. "I respect his privacy. You read the column?"

"Oh, sure. I like the way you write. I was pretty surprised when I saw your byline on the story about Jonathan."

I saw Jonathan glance at Lisa. She was all unaware smiles. I said, "Yeah, me too. I mean, I was surprised to get the assignment. But you've read some of my columns on Jonathan's father, I'm sure."

Lisa looked surprised. "Yeah. Must be weird, right? Writing about Senator Granger and then meeting his son. I can't imagine there's much love lost between you and the Senator. I mean, you're gay, right?"

"As a parade." I looked at Jonathan, who was blushing.

"Very brave of you to be so upfront about it," Lisa said.

I was done with the small talk. "Lisa, do you mind if I borrow your date for a moment? I just need a word. I promise to return him in one piece."

"Sure. I'll go find the ladies' room."

When she was gone, I said, "So. She seems nice."

"Yeah," said Jonathan. "She's really great. But I, uh...." He trailed off. He seemed to know better than to lie to me. He could have given me some song and dance about how they got along well and he really saw a future with her, but instead he stopped talking.

"I wasn't sure if I should come over here at all." I looked around to make sure our reporter friend and the guy with the camera were not nearby. The reporter was harassing someone else a good fifty feet on the other side of the room, well out of earshot. The photographer was shooting overly posed group photos of the cast. To Jonathan, I said, "A reporter at the door bugged me about you. He asked me point blank if I knew if you were gay."

"What did you say?" he asked.

"'No comment'. It's not my place to tell."

I looked at the glass in Jonathan's hand. I figured whatever he was drinking would have a lot of booze in it and that I needed some more liquid courage to carry on this conversation. Without asking permission, I took and drank from it. It did not taste how I expected. "Either the bartender is very good or there's no rum in this Coke."

"No rum," he said. "Once I saw you were here, I decided I needed to keep my wits about me in case I got the chance to talk to you."

"Smart thinking. Was there something specific you wanted to talk to me about?"

"No, I guess not. Why did you come over here?"

"I couldn't stay away."

And then we both looked at our feet.

I took a deep breath as I studied his shoes. They looked expensive and new. I wondered if his father had purchased them. It was as I contemplated how shiny they were that I realized I had no idea what to say.

"I figured you'd be here," he said. He shifted his feet.

I looked up at him. What I said next I said mostly to the top of his head. I lowered my voice to keep the conversation between us. I decided to just tell him the truth. "I've wanted to call you every day since the last time we talked. I've considered caving in. I've missed you like crazy. And I thought, eh, whatever, my boyfriend doesn't need to be out, as long as we get to spend time together."

"Drew...."

"But that's crazy talk, right? I'd ultimately find that frustrating. I mean, I've given this a lot of thought over the last couple of weeks. I think this problem with us is not just about the Senator. It's about you. If you can't find a way to reconcile who you are with who you think you should be, well, we'd never have a real relationship and I'd grow resentful and everything would fall apart. Right?"

He didn't say anything. His gaze settled somewhere near the middle of my chest, like he was trying to interpret the pattern of little squiggles on my tie.

"Or maybe I wouldn't," I said. "Maybe given enough time, you'd figure it out, and we'd deal with the Senator together. We'd lay low until after the campaign. Maybe it would be enough just for us to be together. To have someone to come home to." I stopped to listen to the music that was playing and hummed a few bars. "Ha, Cole Porter." I had always liked Cole Porter, and it was a fitting song: "You'd Be So Nice to Come Home To." I sang along for a couple of lines.

Jonathan just stood there and stared at me. I thought maybe I was off key. I had a passable singing voice, I thought, but not an exceptional one.

"He wrote this song for one of his male lovers, you know," I said. "A choreographer, I think."

"I didn't know."

"'You'd be so nice, you'd be paradise, to come home to and love'," I sang.

Jonathan continued to stare and then said, "How could anyone not fall in love with you?"

"What?"

"When you sing like that. How is it possible for anyone to resist you?"

Well, gee. "Are you saying that singing a few Cole Porter lyrics is the secret way to your heart?"

Jonathan laughed softly and shook his head. "You found the secret way to my heart weeks ago. Man, I've missed the hell out of you too."

"Then why did you leave me?"

He glanced around the room. "I took the coward's way out, I guess. All I ever wanted was for you to have everything you deserve. I care about you, you know. I wanted you to be happy. I didn't think I could give you what you wanted, so I chose to give you the chance to find it with somebody who could."

I bent my head slightly so that I could speak without being overheard. "*You* are what I want."

Jonathan smiled briefly, but he said, "At what cost? You just said yourself, you'd grow to resent me, and then neither of us are happy."

"So what are we going to do?"

He made a low guttural noise, speaking to his own frustration. I felt that, too, in my gut. It was ineffable. It was *impossible*.

He said, "I honestly don't know what's best here. But I guess the ball's kind of in my court, right? I have to choose. Do I choose love or do I choose the easy way."

"Love?"

"I think you'd be pretty nice to come home to."

It was my turn to smile.

"Do you love me?" Jonathan asked.

"Yes." I didn't even have to think about it. I knew. I'd been living with the ache of his absence for all those weeks. And then, there he was, standing right there, and I still couldn't have him, and it was breaking me. That was some powerful stuff right there.

Jonathan nodded.

"You don't have to decide now," I said, figuring this was a conversation that probably should not have been conducted in public, closets or not. "There's a lot of press here, and Lisa, and I understand if you don't want to—"

"You're just going to keep throwing yourself on that sword, aren't you?" Jonathan asked.

"What?"

"You're supposed to get mad. You're supposed to fight for what you want, what you need. Tell me to fuck off, have that be the end of it. Stop making excuses for me."

"I don't get it."

"Walking away was really difficult." He looked down and shook his head. "I've missed you so much. Saying good bye gets harder every time."

I took a step back, my hands on my hips. I scanned the crowd. The reporter had spotted us and was inching closer. I saw him motion to the photographer. On the other side of the room, I saw Lisa come out of the ladies' room and start walking towards us. It was starting to feel like the room was shrinking.

Then what Jonathan had been saying clicked, and I looked back at him. "You need the ultimatum," I said. "It's harder for you to say goodbye because it's not what you want, and I make it worse by lingering, by letting you get away with it. You stick around but feel guilty about it, so then you begin to resent me. Right?"

"Maybe."

"I understand now. You need me to walk away because you're not capable of doing it again." I think that was when I started to feel the anger Jonathan needed me to feel. Except then a very strange idea popped into my head, so instead of leaving, I leaned forward again and whispered, "You know, if you really loved me, you'd fight for me. You'd send that 'fuck you' to your father. You could do something really radical like kiss me right here in front of that photographer. He and the reporter, the guy with the silver-rimmed glasses and the dark hair over there, they both know who we are."

"You know I can't do that," he said under his breath. He was looking to his right, so I followed his gaze and saw Lisa back nearby.

So I nodded. "I figured it was worth a shot. You're right, it is your choice. Love or misery. Doesn't seem that hard to me." I turned. "Nice knowing you, Jonathan."

I don't know why I'm such a fucking martyr sometimes, but I basically decided that my final gift to him would be the out he needed. If I was pissed, he'd feel less bad about ending things.

Behind me, I heard Lisa say, "What was all that about?"

Jonathan replied, "Lisa, I am terribly sorry."

"For what?"

"For what I'm about to do. I should have told you before I brought you to this party. Hell, I should have told you two months ago."

"Told me what?"

He didn't answer. "Drew!" he called instead.

My shoulders tightened involuntarily, although there was a little trickle of something happy working its way through my chest, because something in me knew what he was about to do.

When I turned around, I saw that the reporter and the photographer were definitely interested in us now. I waited for Jonathan to close the gap between us, and he did, grabbing the lapels of my suit jacket. Then he pulled me to him and kissed me. And not just kissed me, but big, open-mouthed, sloppy kissed me, and the whole world stopped.

I saw flashbulbs pop in my peripheral vision. Then I felt Jonathan sigh into my mouth, and still we kept on kissing, as people around us noticed and started murmuring. There was applause, even. It might have been one of the greatest kisses of all time.

And that was it. For better or for worse, Jonathan had made his choice.

And I started crying because I'm a big baby. I tried laughing to cover it up. "I always thought that whole 'if you love someone, set them free' thing was bullshit," I said, trying for a joke. I pulled him into my arms just to feel him there, to make sure all this was real.

Lisa cleared her throat. Jonathan pulled away slightly and looked over at her, his eyes wide, though his fingers were still wrapped around the lapels of my jacket.

"Well," she said. "I guess that explains a lot."

"Lisa," Jonathan said. "I'm so sorry... I didn't mean for... this is not what I had planned. I really thought that you and I could... but now...." He frowned. "I'm so sorry."

She smiled sadly. "It's okay. When you said you were seeing someone, this is who you meant, wasn't it?"

Jonathan nodded. I put my arms around him and pulled him close. The way we came together felt like coming home. He put his arms around my back and pressed his face into my shoulder, so I bent my head and inhaled, smelling him and his shampoo, and it was all so comforting and familiar.

"How could anyone not fall in love with you?" I whispered in his ear. "I was kidding when I made that suggestion. I was just hoping to get a reaction out of you. I never thought you would really—"

"It wasn't a hard decision," he said. "Like you said, love or misery. I choose love. You changed my whole life, Drew. I can't go back to living the way that I was, not when I've seen how things can be. Although I can hear my bank account draining. I'm pretty sure I just got disinherited."

"Feh, money. You can crash with me and eat ramen for awhile. Hell, you can be my kept man if you keep kissing me like that."

He laughed. "I can do that."

I looked up and scanned the room again. Jonathan seemed to burrow deeper into my shoulder. "Things are about to get a little crazy," I said, loud enough for Lisa to hear too. To Jonathan, I whispered, "Before they do, I just want to say that I love you and you're totally insane and I love you some more."

He laughed into my shoulder. "I love you too," he said, his voice muffled. "So much."

"Then all is right in the world."

That was when the room collapsed on us. The reporter, the photographer, even casual observers, everyone had questions. "Mr. Granger! Mr. Walsh! What does this mean? Are you really gay? Is this your official coming out? Are you a couple? How long have you been together? What does Senator Granger think of all this? He's come out against gay marriage, how does that make you feel?"

Jonathan looked around, bewildered. I just laughed and held him close.

"THANKS for ruining my party, *Andrew*," Rey said after pulling me, Jonathan, and Lisa into the back room. The cast of the show had been using this little anteroom—with its own bar, I should add—as a place to hide out from the crowds. Rey had come out to rescue us when things looked like they might go south, but by the time he was able to extract us from the teeming horde, there wasn't much of a horde left.

"I had nothing to do with this, *Reynolds*," I said. "Talk to your cousin, he's the one who kissed me in front of all those people. Besides, nothing's ruined. This is the best party I've ever been to."

While it was true that I hadn't stopped grinning since Jonathan had kissed me in front of one hundred people and the press, it was also true that the press's attention was most definitely not on the show we were all there to celebrate, as Rey had reminded Jonathan about six times on the walk to the back room.

"Jesus, those reporters are like fucking piranhas," Jonathan said, shaking his hand as if one had bit him.

"What did you expect?" Rey asked.

"I don't know. I thought there'd be a small commotion, then people would move on. Or, no, actually, I wasn't thinking."

I put my arms around Jonathan from behind, resting my chin on his shoulder. "Can I take him home now?"

Rey glanced back at the crowd. "You really want to push through that again?"

"Isn't there a back door or something?" Jonathan asked.

"I checked my coat in the front," I said. "I don't want to leave it. I really like that coat." I extricated myself from Jonathan and walked over to Rey, looking out at the throng of people. "Hmm. Maybe if we kind of went to the right of the dance floor, then cut in front of the bar?"

Rey grunted and turned his attention to Lisa. "I'm Rey."

"I know. I'm Lisa. I have to say, I never imagined meeting you under circumstances like this. Or, well, meeting you at all."

Rey smiled. "So you're a fan of the show?"

"Stop flirting, Rey," I said. "I need your help to figure this out."

"Lisa—" Jonathan started to say.

"Stop apologizing," she said, waving her hand. "I understand. No hard feelings, I promise. And I get why you need to get out of here now. But this is a glamorous party, so I hope you don't mind if I stick around."

"No, I... wow, okay. Yeah. Thanks."

She nodded. "You can take me out to dinner next week to make up for this and give me the whole sordid story then. I have to say, I'm dead curious." She smiled, then anticipated Jonathan's next question. "I swear, not a word to anyone at school."

Jonathan nodded. "Not that it matters. Half the known world will know about this on Monday." He sighed. "You are wonderful, Lisa. If circumstances were different...." She waved him off again, and he turned to me. "You know, Drew, that reporter is from a TV network, not an entertainment show. We could grant an interview."

"And say what?" I asked.

"I don't know. 'I'm gay'. That's how this coming out thing works, right?"

Rey rolled his eyes, but I thought that was about right. I cupped Jonathan's face in my hands and kissed him again.

Lisa laughed. "Get a room!"

"Gladly," I said.

A cell phone rang. I recognized Jonathan's ringtone. He pulled his phone out of his pocket. "Ah, news travels fast. That would be Dear Old Dad."

"Are you going to answer it?" I asked.

"Nope. Let him sweat a little bit."

Rey looked at us both. "I should be more mad than I am," he said. "It remains to be seen how the publicity plays out. If big things happen at cast parties for the show, you think that will get us more viewers?" He shrugged. "Whatever, I guess I'm happy for you guys."

"You guess?" I asked.

"That was a pretty reckless thing you just did," Rey said to Jonathan. "Why did you do it?"

"I'm not entirely sure," Jonathan said. "I had a choice to make. I could let my father keep winning, I could continue to live in fear, or I could choose what made me happy. I chose happiness. Let the Senator deal with the fallout."

"All right, now we really have to go, or I'm going to just throw you against a wall and have my way with you in front of everyone here," I said.

Jonathan laughed but then looked serious. "Okay," he said. "Let's go."

I smiled and took his hand. Jonathan looked down at our intertwined fingers with an expression of awe on his face. Then we walked out together.

KATE MCMURRAY is a nonfiction editor by day. Among other things, Kate is crafty (mostly knitting and sewing, but she also wields power tools), she plays the violin, she has an English degree, and she loves baseball. She lives in Brooklyn, NY.

Visit her web site at http://www.katemcmurray.com.

Also from KATE MCMURRAY

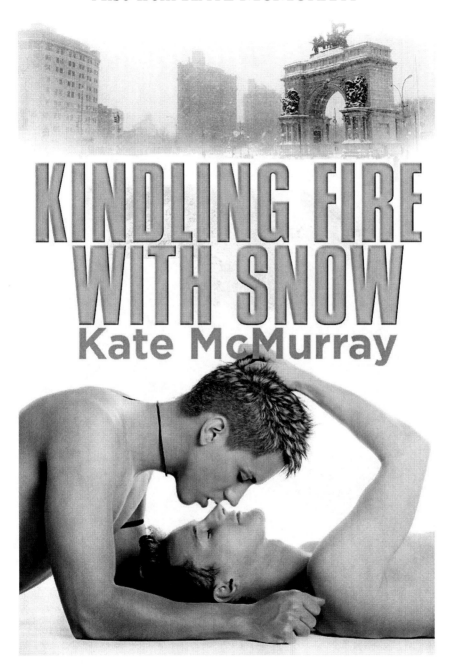

KINDLING FIRE
WITH SNOW
Kate McMurray

http://www.dreamspinnerpress.com